Also by Alex Morgan

THE KICKS SERIES

SAVING THE TEAM

SABOTAGE SEASON

WIN OR LOSE

HAT TRICK

SHAKEN UP

SETTLE THE SCORE

UNDER PRESSURE

IN THE ZONE


BREAKAWAY

# ALEX MORGAN

Simon & Schuster Books for Young Readers
New York  London  Toronto  Sydney  New Delhi

SIMON & SCHUSTER BOOKS FOR YOUNG READERS
An imprint of Simon & Schuster Children's Publishing Division
1230 Avenue of the Americas, New York, New York 10020

SIMON & SCHUSTER BOOKS FOR YOUNG READERS
is a trademark of Simon & Schuster, Inc.
For information about special discounts for bulk purchases, please contact Simon & Schuster Special Sales at 1-866-506-1949 or business@simonandschuster.com.
The Simon & Schuster Speakers Bureau can bring authors to your live event. For more information or to book an event, contact the Simon & Schuster Speakers Bureau at 1-866-248-3049 or visit our website at www.simonspeakers.com.
Book design by Krista Vossen
The text for this book was set in Berling.
Manufactured in the United States of America
0818 FFG
First Edition
2 4 6 8 10 9 7 5 3 1
Library of Congress Cataloging-in-Publication Data
Names: Morgan, Alex (Alexandra Patricia), 1989- author.
Title: Choosing sides / Alex Morgan.
Description: First edition. | New York : Simon & Schuster Books for Young Readers, [2018]
Series: The Kicks | Summary: Devin has to deal with some contention between members of her team, the Kicks, and hostility toward their rivals, the Roses.
Identifiers: LCCN 2017051750 | ISBN 9781481481564 (hardcover)
ISBN 9781481481571 (pbk.) | ISBN 9781481481588 (ebook)
Subjects: | CYAC: Soccer—Fiction. | Conduct of life—Fiction.
Friendship—Fiction. | Middle schools—Fiction. | Schools—Fiction.
Classification: LCC PZ7.M818 Cho 2018 | DDC [Fic]—dc23
LC record available at https://lccn.loc.gov/2017051750

# CHAPTER ONE

*We are not a team because we work together. We are a team because we respect, trust, and care for one another.*

I found this meme one night when I was randomly searching for teamwork on the Internet, because that is something I do sometimes. Maybe that sounds silly, but I do it to get inspiration. And this quote inspired me, so I made it my cell phone wallpaper, with a background of the U.S. Women's National Soccer team in a huddle.

Not long after I found it, I discovered how true that quote really was, and how bad it could be when a team *wasn't* working together. When I think back about it, I realize that the problem started one day at lunch.

"Heads up, Devin!" a voice called out over the din in the crowded Kentville Middle School cafeteria.

Usually when I heard that expression, I was on the soccer field, ready to pounce on the ball that was coming my way. At the moment it wasn't a soccer ball sailing toward me; it was a wadded-up piece of paper.

As I caught the paper in my right hand, I looked up and saw my friend Steven grinning at me.

"Good catch!" He gave me a thumbs-up. "Those are my notes for the World Civ test. Carlo took it during third period, and he said it's a killer. You might want to do some studying during lunch." Then he shrugged. "Not that you need it. You usually ace your tests."

"Thanks." I smiled back at him. " I'll check them out. You can never be too prepared. See you later," I said as his friend Cody began calling his name, waving him over to an empty seat.

"Bye." Steven smiled at me again before running over to join Cody. Both of them were on the boys' soccer team at Kentville, and the team members usually all sat together.

That was who I was sitting with too, my bffs and soccer teammates. Officially we were the Kentville Kangaroos, but everyone called us the Kicks. Middle school could be a social nightmare, and so I was really glad that I had a team to sit with. *My* team.

Sitting on my right was Emma. Her family was Korean, and on most days her mom liked to pack her a totally tasty and loaded lunch: pickled vegetables, rice, chicken or some other protein, and fruit. It always looked so good, and Emma was so sweet that she regularly brought an extra pair of chopsticks in case someone wanted to dive into her bento box and try something new. Emma was the tallest member of the Kicks and the team goalie. She wore her long, black hair in a ponytail, and she was dressed casually in jeans and a T-shirt.

Zoe, sitting next to Emma, hovered her chopsticks over the food-filled compartments of the bento box. The shortest person at the table, Zoe was fast and feisty on the field. Off the field she was a true fashionista. That day, she wore a mustard-yellow cropped sweater with a black-and-white tartan-print short skirt. I would look like a clown if I ever attempted the prints that Zoe wore, but she always looked super-chic. She'd been growing out her strawberry-blond hair, and now it was long enough for her to tuck behind her ears.

"I can't decide!" Zoe sighed as she contemplated all of Emma's lunch treats.

"Mom made veggie bibimbap," Emma said. "I know it's your favorite."

"The first day we met, I tried your mom's bibimbap," Zoe reminded her. "And that was all the way back in kindergarten!"

"I never knew if you liked me for me or for my mom's cooking," Emma teased, and Zoe gave her shy smile that I had come to know so well.

"Maybe it was a little bit of both," she replied with a laugh.

"No bibimbap for you!" Emma pretended to pout as she grabbed the bento box and turned away from Zoe.

"If you don't want it, I'll have it!" Jessi exclaimed. "I

don't know what's in this salad my mom packed for me, but it tastes so bitter. Blech!" She stuck her tongue out.

Zoe grabbed a green leaf and nibbled. "Tastes like kale," she said.

In the seat next to me on my left, Jessi rolled her eyes. "I think she's spending too much time with your mom, Devin. First she confiscates all of my hot Cheetos. Now kale salad! It's not natural!"

We all burst out laughing. Everyone knew that my mom was a total health-food nut, and she and Mrs. Dukes, Jessi's mom, were becoming friends. Which was awesome, because Jessi had been my first good friend when I had first moved to Kentville, California, from Connecticut. I'll never forget how nervous I was the first day of school. Meeting Jessi, Emma, Zoe, and Frida had made me feel not so alone.

Jessi was a midfielder. Today she wore her black hair in a cascade of bouncy curls. Jessi was high energy, on and off the field, and was always a lot of fun.

"Kale is a natural food, unlike disgusting processed snack foods." Frida tossed her auburn hair over her shoulder as she spoke. My most dramatic friend, Frida, was an actress who usually pretended to be a character while on the soccer field. She'd been everything from a spy, to a princess, to an Amazon warrior. It totally confused the opposing team, especially when she shouted things like "Princess power!"

"You're an athlete," Frida continued. "You need to eat healthy, whole foods. That's why I'm going on an organic, gluten-free diet. It's great for the skin."

"Why, so you'll look fabulous on camera?" Jessi wondered "Do you have a new starring role?"

Frida had acted in a TV movie called *Mall Mania* and in several commercials. That was another big difference about living in California. None of my Connecticut friends were TV stars!

Frida beamed. "I thought you'd never ask," she said. "I've got some exciting news! I'm the lead in the local theater production of the *Mystery Date* musical."

"*Mystery Date*? Is that, like, a thriller?" Emma asked.

"No, it's a board game from the sixties and seventies," Frida replied.

"Yeah," Zoe chimed in. "It's this game where you try to get the best date while avoiding the dud. If you get the dud, you lose."

"How do you know that?" Jessi asked her.

"My mom had it when she was a kid, and she saved it," Zoe replied. "My older sisters love to play it. I'd rather play Monopoly."

"Wait. I still don't get how they could make a musical out of a board game," Emma said.

"Musicals can be inspired by almost anything," Frida said. "There are no rules to creativity."

Jessi shook her head. "Seriously? Have they turned checkers into a musical too?"

"No, but there was an award-winning musical about chess," Frida replied.

I was less concerned about the creative source of

Frida's musical than I was about her schedule.

"Are you sure you have time to do all those play rehearsals?" I asked, thinking about soccer practice. "We're right in the middle of the spring season, and we're on track for the semifinals."

"Don't worry, Devin." Frida waved her hand as if waving away my concerns. "I know it will take a lot of effort on my part to honor all of my commitments, but Miriam told me that live theater is exactly what I need to hone my craft."

Miriam was a famous (and very old) actress who had starred in a lot of black-and-white movies. We had met her at a nursing home where we'd all been volunteering. Miriam and Frida had hit it off and had kept in touch ever since. They were both divas at heart, and it explained why Frida had been talking less like a seventh grader and more like a seventy-year-old lately.

"Tomorrow we're playing the Santa Flora Roses," Jessi added. "Not much to worry about there. They are the weakest team in the league!"

"Yes, tomorrow's game should be a snap," Zoe said.

Emma sighed. "I can't believe I almost gave up soccer for good! If it weren't for all of you, I never would have played again."

Jessi reached across the table and patted Emma's arm. "The Kicks wouldn't be the same without you. So what if your cleat flew off during a game and banged you smack in the forehead? It could happen to anyone."

"Jessi, you know that my flying shoe wasn't the

problem—it was that somebody took a picture right when the shoe hit me in the head, and then I became a meme sensation," she said with a groan. Then she started to giggle. "Looking back, I can see how funny it was. At the time, not so much!"

"I'm glad you're back to your old self, Emma," I chimed in. "Santa Flora might be an easy win tomorrow, but we'll need you in the goal if we want to get to the semifinals."

"I'm all in!" Emma said. "What's everyone up to after the game tomorrow?"

Jessi smiled. "Devin and I are going bowling with Cody and Steven tomorrow night. I can't wait to see the look on Cody's face when I demolish him."

Jessi could be really competitive when it came to Cody. At the mention of our bowling night, I got a big smile on my face. I wasn't allowed to date, and neither was Jessi, but we were allowed to hang out in groups with some of our guy friends. I was kind of crushing on Steven, and Jessi had also been crushing on Cody, but things had gotten a little weird when Jessi had made a new friend named Sebastian. I wasn't sure if Jessi still had a crush on Cody or if they were just good friends, but I was glad that the four of us could start hanging out together again. We always had so much fun.

"Well." Emma put her chopsticks down and beamed happily. "Zoe and I are going to be attending the first ever in-person county fan club meeting for the Real McCoys!" she squealed.

"Wait, is Brady McCoy going to be there?" Jessi asked, sounding confused. Brady was Emma's favorite pop star. He had starred in *Mall Mania* with Frida, and thanks to her, Emma had had the chance to meet her idol in person. "Haven't you already met him? I thought maybe after that you would have cooled down a little bit, you know?"

"I am still obsessed with Brady," Emma admitted. "But this is just a meeting of the fan club. It's cool because we've only ever communicated with one another online. Now I finally get to meet some of my favorite peeps, like BradyLover4Ever and McCoyest, in person! We're both so excited. Right, Zoe?"

Zoe stared blankly at the piece of mushroom trapped between her chopsticks, before shrugging and placing the chopsticks down. "I told you I wasn't sure if I could make it. I have other plans," Zoe said softly.

Emma laughed. "You're kidding, right? What could be more important? Besides, you are almost as crazy about Brady McCoy as I am."

Zoe sighed and shrugged again, but Emma acted like she didn't notice.

"We're going to watch his concert video for his second album, *Brady's Back*," Emma said. "I can't wait! McCoyest has the director's cut with special, never-before-seen behind-the-scenes footage. It's going to be totally amazing!"

Emma kept talking about the fan club thing, while Zoe kept looking down at the table, frowning. Emma's enthusiasm about Brady could be exhausting, and it looked like it was starting to get to Zoe.

I didn't care if Emma talked about Brady McCoy for hours, as long as she brought that energy with her onto the soccer field. If she did that, the Kicks would have a clear shot at the semifinals! So I tuned out Emma. But sometimes I wonder, if I had been paying more attention that day at lunch, if I could have helped to prevent a crisis—a crisis like the Kicks had never seen before.

# CHAPTER TWO

I hopped up and down on the Kicks field, warming up my legs and stretching. Not only were the Roses currently last in the league, but the Kicks also had the home-field advantage. I wasn't stressed about the game, but there was no way I was going to get overconfident. For all we knew, the Roses might have been practicing really hard, or had learned some new plays. You never could tell. I was determined to stay on my toes and not let my guard down.

"Go, Devin!" my mom yelled from the stands. Normally my dad and my little sister, Maisie, would be with Mom, but Maisie was on her elementary school soccer team, and my dad had volunteered to coach.

I thought Maisie might have ended up hating soccer because our parents had been dragging her to my games ever since she was a baby. Instead it had inspired her to play, and I had to admit she was pretty good at it. On this

Saturday morning her team had a game at the same time as mine. My mom had insisted on coming to my game, even though I'd told her she didn't have to.

"Devin, there will always be one member of the Burke family there to cheer you on," Mom had said. "Even if you end up playing for years and going pro."

"Pro? Me?" I had said. Of course I had thought of it before—but in that daydream kind of way, where you imagine yourself in a huge stadium and your fans are doing the wave. But I hadn't seriously thought about making a career out of playing soccer, not until Mom had said those words. Usually I thought about being a teacher, or maybe a physical therapist or something like that.

I must have had a slightly panicked look on my face, because then Mom had said, "Oh, no pressure, Devin! I was just trying to encourage you. I think you have the drive to become anything you want to be in life."

Now I looked up and saw Mom's face in the stands, and I wanted to make her proud. And I also wanted to figure out something for myself: Was being a pro soccer player something I could accomplish? Was it something I *wanted* to accomplish?

Then I heard my co-captain, Grace, call out, "Sock swap!" I had brought the pregame ritual with me from Connecticut, and my new teammates had liked it—even Grace and the other eighth graders, who hadn't wanted a newcomer to come in and start changing things right away.

I ran to join my teammates, and we all got into a circle and sat down on the grass. Since Coach Flores didn't make us wear uniform socks, we could wear whatever crazy pattern we wanted to. For the sock swap we passed one sock to the teammate on our right, and the result was that nobody on the field wore matching socks. It made the Kicks unique and always raised our spirits before a game.

Zoe passed me her sock, a pretty one with cherry blossom flowers going up the leg, with bands of deep burgundy at the top and toes.

"Wow, nice sock, Zoe!" I said.

Jessi held up a black sock with rows of garden gnomes running up the legs. "Look at what Emma is forcing me to wear! Strange little men in funny hats!"

"Garden gnomes are adorable!" Emma protested.

"No way! They're super creepy!" Jessi said. "Didn't you see *Blood Garden: Revenge of the Gnome?*"

"Ew, no!" Emma squealed. "And I never will!"

With our socks and shoes back on, everyone on the team jumped up and put a hand into the center of the circle.

"Gooooo, Kicks!" we cheered.

Coach Flores approached us, with her curly brown hair pulled into a ponytail. She wore a Windbreaker in Kicks blue, along with her usual smile. Coach Flores usually looked happy. If she wasn't, something was very, very wrong.

"All right, girls. Go out there and do your best," she said. "When we do our best, we never lose."

Then she announced the game lineup. "Zarine, you're starting on goal. Sarah, Anjali, Jade, and Frida, you're defense. Jessi, Taylor, Anna, you're my midfield. Devin, Hailey, Grace, I want you on forward."

I ran onto the field, ready to face off against the Santa Flora Roses. Yes, we had beaten them in the fall season. And they had the worst record in our division. But the Kicks had been underdogs before too. When I'd first joined the Kicks, the team had been in last place and totally disorganized. When we had come together as a team, everything had changed, and we'd even made it to the state championships! So I knew that sometimes underdogs *could* win.

The California sun shone down onto the field as I waited for the game to start, and I wondered what the delay was. The Roses coach was out on the field, trying to get the girls into position. She looked pretty young—almost like a college student. She had short brown hair, serious-looking black eyeglasses, and a confused look on her face.

I figured she was confused because she had two forwards, two midfielders, and six defenders on the field, which was not a really smart formation. One of the girls ran up to the coach and said something to her, and then the coach started waving at the defenders. All six of them ran up to the midfield, but she sent four of them back and told one girl to go into the midfield, and another to play forward.

"But I've never played forward! I'm always on defense!" the girl told her.

"Don't worry. You'll do fine," the coach reassured her. "It's good to try new experiences, right?"

The girl frowned and took her place, and that was when I noticed that all of the Roses were frowning.

"Um, good luck, Roses!" their coach called out. Then she nodded to the ref, and the game finally started.

The Roses' pregame disorganization spilled into the rest of the game, right along with their frowning faces. We ran circles around them from the start and scored two goals in the first ten minutes.

One of the Roses got the ball and started to dance through our defense, but Frida quickly stole the ball from her.

"No time travelers in the red zone!" Frida yelled, and she shot the ball down the field. I had no idea what character she was playing, but I didn't care, as long as she got the job done.

The Roses forward whom Frida had intercepted slumped her shoulders in despair as she jogged back to the center of the field. I recognized her as Sasha, one of my teammates from the Griffons, the winter league team I had played on.

It bothered me to see Sasha looking so defeated, but I didn't have time to dwell on it, because Grace passed the ball to me. I dribbled down the field and blew right by the slow Roses defenders. It wasn't even a challenge. I had a clear shot at the goal, and I sent the ball flying toward the net. I grimaced, because it looked like I had kicked the goal right into the goalie's hands. But it brushed past her fingertips and slammed into the net.

My teammates cheered, but the usual thrill I felt when scoring a goal was kind of muted. I hadn't had to work for it. I felt guilty when the next thought flashed through my mind, but I felt like I could have been playing against Maisie's elementary school team.

The Roses didn't improve as the game went on. I spent some time on the bench, and I watched Sasha. A headband held back her wispy blond hair, and her mouth was set in a firm line of determination as she played. On the Griffons she had been one of our coach's favorite players, with an aggressive playing style that had earned her a lot of fouls, until she'd calmed down. We hadn't gotten along great at first, but by the end of the season we'd been friends.

On the field now, Sasha never stopped hustling. She kept running after the ball. At one point she used some nice footwork to get past Frida and then sent the ball flying over Emma's head and into the net. But it was the only goal the Roses scored all game.

When the final whistle blew, the Kicks had won 10–1. We gathered together for victory hugs and slaps on the back, but none of us were feeling too good about this win.

"They remind me of us at the start of the fall season," Jessi said, shaking her head. "I feel really bad for them."

"Me too," I sighed. "Come on. Let's go shake hands with them."

The other Kicks were walking up to the line of Roses, and I started shaking hands.

"Good game, good game," I said to all the players I shook hands with. Most of them looked down and didn't even make eye contact. Then I came to Sasha.

"Hey, Sasha," I said gently as I offered her my hand. "That was tough out there."

Sasha looked up at me, her hazel eyes brimming with tears. She nodded without saying anything. I had the feeling that if she'd tried to talk, she would have burst out crying.

"Look, I know what it's like." I wanted to say something, anything that would make her feel better. "The Kicks used to be the same exact way. It was so frustrating. But we got better. I know the Roses can too."

Sasha gave a gulp as if she were swallowing her tears. "Thanks," she said in a voice that was just a little louder than a whisper.

I made my way down the rest of the line. When I was finished, Jessi was waiting for me.

"My mom said we'll pick you up at six. Okay?" she asked.

"Can't wait!" I said as Jessi darted away to meet her mom.

Mrs. Dukes was expecting a baby. Her stomach was starting to look really big, like she had a soccer ball tucked into her shirt. I wondered if Jessi was going to have a little brother or a little sister. Mr. and Mrs. Dukes knew, but they were keeping it a surprise. Jessi couldn't wait to find out, because she really wanted a little sister. I told her she could have Maisie anytime.

As I went looking for my mom, I felt a tap on my shoulder. I twirled around to see Sasha behind me.

"I really miss playing with you on the Griffons," Sasha said. "Coach Darby was tough, but I didn't mind. At least she helped us win games. When our old coach retired, we got stuck with Coach Doyle, who's never played soccer in her life. She's constantly saying stuff like how soccer 'builds character,' and she doesn't care if we win, as long as we do our best. But I care about winning, and I'm not the only one."

She looked so sad and angry at the same time. I knew exactly how she felt.

"I totally get it," I said sympathetically. "Coach Flores used to be the same way."

"Really?" Sasha asked. "Because I can't believe that anyone could be as disorganized as Coach Doyle. You should have seen her handing out positions at the start of the game. 'Who feels like playing forward? Who wants to play defense?' It was total chaos."

I nodded. "It sounds like she just wants to make sure that everyone has a fair chance. Coach Flores used to do the same thing. She still makes sure everyone has game time and gets to try positions they're interested in, but now she has a lot more strategy when it comes to games."

"How did you fix it? What changed?" Sasha asked eagerly.

"A lot of things," I said. "First we had to let Coach Flores know that we wanted to win. Then we had to get all of our teammates on board. And we did a lot of team building exercises."

Just then I heard my mom calling me. "Devin! Let's go!"

"I gotta go," I said to Sasha, who frowned. "Hey, here's my cell phone number." I told her the digits and she keyed them into her phone. "Feel free to text if you need anything. Good luck!"

"Thanks, Devin," she said, and I jogged off the field and toward the parking lot, where my mom was waiting for me.

"Great game, sweetie," she said. "Now I've got some good news and some bad news. The good news is that Maisie's team won their game too, and Dad and I are taking you both out to lunch to celebrate. We're going to meet Dad and Maisie at the restaurant."

"Ugh!" I groaned. I knew what was coming next. "Don't tell me. The bad news is that we're going to Pirate Pete's."

Mom laughed. "It *is* Maisie's turn to pick."

*There are worse things*, I thought. *I'd rather be celebrating a win at Maisie's favorite, corny pirate-themed restaurant than going home feeling totally hopeless like poor Sasha!*

# CHAPTER THREE

I survived Pirate Pete's, and later that night Jessi and I sang along to our new favorite song as her mom drove us to meet Steven and Cody at Loaded Lanes, a bowling alley that had cool laser lights, a full arcade, and all kinds of yummy food that a waiter would bring to you while you bowled.

"I'll see you in the headlines." Jessi crooned the last line of the song while I sang backup.

As the song ended, Mrs. Dukes said, "I'm impressed. Sure you two don't want to give up soccer and join the school's chorus instead?"

"No thanks!" Jessi said immediately and emphatically. "I'll stick to singing in the shower."

I laughed. "Right. Soccer comes first!"

"Although, Sebastian is in chorus," Jessi said with a sly smile. "He's got a really great voice."

"I'll have to go to the spring concert, then," I said. "Are you going?"

Jessi nodded. "Sebastian wants to go out for ice cream afterward."

"I'm so glad you figured out a way to be friends with both Sebastian and Cody," I said. Part of why I was so happy was because Cody and Steven were best friends, and I wouldn't see Steven as much if Jessi and Cody weren't friends too. But I didn't want to say that part out loud in front of Mrs. Dukes.

"Me too!" Jessi grinned.

"Me three!" Mrs. Dukes chimed. "You are both too young for this boyfriend stuff."

Jessi rolled her eyes. "I know, I know. We're all *just friends*. And it's not like I'm going to have much of a social life soon, after my baby brother or sister comes."

Mrs. Dukes laughed at that. "I think my social life will be way more on hold than yours, Jessi."

"I told you I am totally going to help you out," Jessi reminded her mom.

"Yes, and I appreciate that. But you still need to have fun and do things with your friends," Mrs. Dukes replied.

"When is the baby due?" I asked.

"In about six weeks," answered Mrs. Dukes. "And in case he or she comes early, we are all ready. The room is done and we've got everything set up."

"Yes, and I am all moved into my closet," Jessi joked. She'd had to give up her room for the baby, and the room she'd moved into was a lot smaller than her old one.

"You are already an amazing and kind big sister, and your sibling hasn't even been born yet," Mrs. Dukes said, not taking the bait. Then she pulled up in front of Loaded Lanes.

"I'll pick you up at nine," she told us. "If you want to come home earlier, just give me a call."

"Thanks, Mom!" Jessi said, and I said "Thanks, Mrs. Dukes!" simultaneously as we got out of the car. We headed into the bowling alley, and Jessi glanced down at her phone.

"Cody and Steven are here. They've got a lane reserved for us," she said as we walked in.

"Over here!" Cody called from a lane. He waved an arm in the air, a smile spreading across his face. Steven stood beside him, smiling and waving too.

"We'll be right there!" Jessi called. "Let's get our shoes."

We got in line to rent our bowling shoes. It was a busy night, and lots of people were bowling. The place was dark, with colorful lights reflecting off the gleaming lanes. Sound effects blared from the video games in the arcade, and music blasted through the speakers near the lanes. I smiled. It was going to be a fun night!

We got our hideous shoes—half red, half blue, with rounded toes—and Jessi laughed. "Do you think Zoe would be caught dead in these?"

I shook my head. "No way. She'd probably refuse to put them on and sit on the bench all night."

We slipped on our ugly shoes and walked over to the lane where Cody and Steven were. Cody's smile grew bigger.

"Are you ready to witness my awesome bowling skills?" he said, and smirked.

Jessi smirked back. "Yes, I'm going to be pretty amazed at how many gutter balls you bowl."

"I'll show *you*!" Cody laughed, and the two of them began bantering back and forth.

Steven grinned at me. "Here we go," he said, and we both laughed. We were used to how Cody and Jessi loved to tease each other.

Then Jessi and I searched the racks to find bowling balls that fit our fingers and weren't too heavy—but weren't too light, either. I found a blue, speckled one that reminded me of the Kicks, so I chose that one. Jessi picked a red ball and then entered our names into the electronic scoreboard: Jessi, Devin, Steven, Cody.

"Aw, how come you get to go first?" Cody complained. "And I'm last?"

Jessi grinned. "Because I got to the scoreboard first," she said. "Now watch and learn."

Jessi got a serious look on her face, and she held up her ball in her right hand, supporting it with her left. Then she did a series of comical, silly steps before throwing her ball, which had all of us cracking up. *Bam!* She knocked down all ten pins.

"Strike!" I cheered.

"Woo-hoo!" she called as she gave me a high five. "Your turn, Devin."

I picked up my ball, feeling a little nervous. I'd only been bowling a few times in my life, usually when my friends in Connecticut had bowling birthday parties. And I hadn't bowled at all since we'd moved to California. So I had a feeling I wasn't going to get a strike.

I held up the ball. I tried to keep my eye on the center pin. I took three steps up to the line, and then I let go. The ball skidded up the middle of the lane . . . and then started to drift right. It drifted all the way into the gutter!

"You're just warming up, Devin!" Jessi encouraged me.

But my second ball was a gutter ball too, and that really bugged me. Even off the soccer field, I was pretty competitive.

"You'll do better next time, Devin," Steven assured me, and then he knocked down seven pins on his turn, which was respectable. After him Cody grabbed his ball with confidence and bowled a strike.

He grinned at Jessi. "You're going to have to hustle to keep up with me," he warned.

"No problem," Jessi said, jumping up. She knocked down eight pins on her first ball, and then got the last two on her second try, for a spare.

"Nice!" I said.

"She's just lucky!" Cody countered.

It was my turn. I got up and frowned. I did not want to throw gutter balls again.

Jessi came up to me. "Keep your wrist straight when you throw," she advised. "You were twisting yours last time." She demonstrated.

"Got it," I said. I stared at the pins, then took two steps up to the line. This time I concentrated on my wrist as I released the ball. The ball zoomed down the middle of the lane, and knocked all but one pin down.

"Yes!" Jessi yelled, and we high-fived again.

Steven grinned, and we slapped palms too.

"I figured you'd be a quick learner," he said.

We took a quick break as a waiter came over to take our order. We all got burgers and fries.

"Does the burger have kale on it?" Jessi asked, and the waiter gave her a strange look.

"No," he said.

"I'll take it!" Jessi told him as she set down her menu, and the rest of us cracked up.

We bowled a few more rounds while waiting for the food to arrive. By the time the waiter came back, I was one point behind Steven, and Jessi and Cody were way ahead of both of us, taking turns claiming the top spot. We had another break to eat, and as we were munching, both Jessi and I got a text message at the same time.

"It's Emma," Jessi said.

I glanced down at my phone and read the text out loud.

Zoe didn't show up for Real McCoys fan club meeting. I tried to text her, but she didn't answer. Is she with you guys? Do you know where she is?

"Real McCoys?" Steven wondered.

"It's a fan club that Emma and Zoe belong to for Brady McCoy," I explained.

"He's so lame," Cody sneered.

Steven shrugged. "Some of his songs are okay."

"You *would* think so. You've got the same haircut," Cody teased him.

Steven pretended to dust off his shoulders. "You're just jealous because I look so good."

Steven used to wear his hair spiky. Now he had his bangs pulled over his forehead in a messy fringe, with the rest trimmed short on the sides. It looked supercute.

Jessi began texting. "I'm letting Emma know that I haven't seen Zoe or heard from her. You?"

"Nope." I shook my head. "You know, Zoe doesn't seem to like Brady McCoy too much anymore. She tried to tell Emma at lunch yesterday that she didn't want to go to the fan club meeting, but Emma wasn't paying attention."

Jessi sighed. "I noticed that too. Zoe and Emma have been friends since kindergarten . . . but things can change."

I nodded. "Yes, but sometimes they stay the same." I couldn't resist teasing Jessi. "After all, you still like *The Sunshine Puppies*."

*The Sunshine Puppies* was a kids' show. When Frida, Emma, Zoe, and I had helped Jessi move out of her old room into her new one, we'd uncovered her stash of DVDs and stuffed animals.

"I stand by my love of the Sunshine Puppies. They

are the cutest, and I am not afraid to admit it," Jessi said proudly.

"What? Sunshine Puppies, seriously? Jessi, I had no idea you were such a dork," Cody teased her.

"I'm a dork and proud of it!" Jessi raised her voice. A couple of the other bowlers looked over at us, and I couldn't help but laugh. They must have thought that Jessi was nuts!

"Um, you really shouldn't talk, Cody," Steven said to his friend. "Isn't there a certain bear named Freddy the Teddy that is still on your bed?"

"Freddy the Teddy? That's hysterical!" Jessi snorted.

Cody, who was usually so confident, actually got a slight red blush on his cheeks. "My grandma gave him to me when I was a baby," he said.

"Cody sleeps with his teddy bear," Jessi started to chime in a singsong voice.

"Freddy the Teddy is more than just a bear. He's a friend," Cody joked.

Jessi kept right on singing. Cody put down his burger and stood up.

"I'm warning you," he said.

Jessi stopped to ask, "What are you going to do?"

Cody smiled. "Chase you all around this bowling alley until you are too tired to sing."

Jessi laughed. "You're on," she said, before she started singing again as she darted away.

Cody started chasing Jessi around Loaded Lanes.

Steven and I looked at each other and shook our heads. "They're both crazy," I said.

"They are. But they make everything fun," Steven agreed.

"True. Jessi is always cracking all of us up." I replied, and when I said "us," it made me think of my other friends. "I hope everything will be okay between Emma and Zoe."

Steven replied, "I'm sure they'll be fine. If Zoe isn't that into Brady McCoy, that shouldn't stop Emma, right?"

Steven made it all sound so simple. I relaxed—until a loud scream filled the air, and I jumped out of my seat.

Cody had grabbed Jessi near the bowling shoe rental booth, and she had let out a bloodcurdling screech. I saw an employee walk over to them. Cody let go of Jessi, and they both grew silent. Then I saw them nod their heads before slowly walking back to the lane.

When they were back, they both dissolved into giggles.

"We almost got kicked out, and it was all your fault, Cody," Jessi laughed.

"My fault? You were the one who screamed!" Cody said.

I grinned. Jessi, Cody, Steven, and I were hanging out like old times. We finished the game, and even the fact that I came in last (by only two points, but who was counting) didn't get me down. I might not have been able to win at bowling, but at least the Kicks were having a winning season!

# CHAPTER FOUR

I lay in bed, stretching slowly as the smell of something delicious cooking for breakfast woke me up. It was such a treat to be able to sleep in. Between school during the week and soccer practices and games on the weekends, sleeping in wasn't something I could do a lot.

I got up and quickly used the bathroom before heading downstairs in my favorite pair of pajamas. The T-shirt said WHAT'S LIFE WITHOUT GOALS? PLAY SOCCER, and the matching pants were black and had little soccer balls all over them.

I breathed in deeply before walking into the kitchen. The smell was so yummy!

"Let me guess? Your world-famous chocolate chip pancakes?" I asked my dad. He stood over the stove, a spatula in his hands.

"Yep, and I got the first one," my sister Maisie said before my dad could answer. She was sitting at the kitchen table, chocolate from the pancakes smeared on her chin.

"Good for you," I replied cheerfully. Then I sat down, and my dad slid a plate of pancakes in front of me. It was too early in the morning to get into an argument with my little sister.

"Here you go, kiddo!" Dad said.

I thanked him and then grabbed the syrup and poured it over my pancakes before digging in. We usually ate very healthfully at home, but every now and then we got a special treat. Dad's pancakes were one of them.

"So, girls, what's on the schedule for today?" Dad asked.

Again Maisie was the first to say something. "Devin promised to do soccer drills with me today!" she said, half-whining. I guess she was expecting me to say no.

"I remember, Maisie," I told her. "Don't worry, we'll do it."

"Yay!" Maisie cheered. "I'm going to watch TV until we start."

She quickly got up from her chair.

"Not so fast!" my dad said. "Go wash up and make your bed first."

"I'll do it later." This time my little sister spoke in full-on whine mode.

My dad gave her that no-nonsense look that meant it was pointless to try to argue with him. At least I had figured that out by now. Maisie, at age eight, was still learning.

"Your hands are sticky from syrup," he said sternly. "And

we do our chores in this household before we watch TV. You know the rules, Maisie."

Instead of arguing, Maisie stomped up the stairs. She was being noisy and annoying about it, but at least she had figured out that arguing was pointless.

*Maybe she has finally learned something,* I thought.

I helped my dad clean up before going upstairs to grab a quick shower and change. Before I got into the shower, I got a text from Sasha, my former teammate on the Griffons who was now on the Santa Flora Roses.

Hey, Devin. U busy today? Can we hang? I'd like to get your advice.

I had plans with Maisie, and I knew I couldn't cancel them. So this was my reply.

If u wanna come hang with me and my little sis, we're doing soccer drills today.

Sasha replied: Cool! What time?

We worked out the details before I jumped into the shower. I was dressed and ready when Sasha rang the doorbell.

"Thanks, Devin, for having me over," she said. "I can't wait to meet your little sister."

I laughed. "You might regret that. Maisie, Sasha's here."

Maisie loved meeting new people and hamming it up in front of them. Usually we had to pry her away from the TV, but I heard it shut off immediately, and she came running in.

"I'm Maisie," she said, beginning to talk excitedly. "Wait

till you see me play. I'm really good. If you want any pointers, let me know."

Maisie charged through the house to the sliding glass doors that led into the backyard. Sasha and I exchanged grins before following her.

"I warned you," I said.

"She's funny," Sasha laughed.

We started out with a simple passing drill, kicking the ball back and forth to Maisie.

"At first I was going to be a forward like Devin, but I think I like playing defense better," Maisie chattered to Sasha happily. "I never let anyone past me. Never!"

I smiled as I thought about the last game of Maisie's that I had seen. One of the players actually had gotten a goal past her, but I didn't say anything.

"Let's do monkey in the middle," Sasha suggested. "I'll be the monkey first. Maisie, you and Devin have to try to pass the ball to each other without letting me get it."

We played for a while, and I noticed how great Sasha was with Maisie, getting her to laugh but focus at the same time.

"I want to be the monkey next!" Maisie said. "But I'm thirsty. I'll be right back! Don't play without me!"

She ran into the house, and Sasha turned to me.

"I've been thinking a lot about what you said after the game yesterday," she said. "I'd really like some more advice. Being on a team that's so disorganized and playing so badly is really bringing me down."

I nodded. "Like I told you yesterday, I completely understand. I was in exactly the same situation you're in. All of the Kicks were."

"You said to talk to Coach Doyle, but that's kind of hard to do," Sasha admitted. "I mean, she really is trying hard to be a good coach, I guess. And we all know that she kind of got stuck with this job. She stepped up to be coach when nobody else wanted to. So I don't want to hurt her feelings."

"I know. But if she's as nice as she sounds, she'll want to help you and your teammates win," I told her. "If you want, I can ask Coach Flores for advice. She might have some ideas of how you can bring it up with your coach."

Sasha's hazel eyes brightened. "That would be so cool. Would you really?"

"Sure. I feel like I can talk to Coach Flores about anything."

Sasha gave me a big hug. "Thanks, Devin!"

I had another idea.

"Did you know that there's a soccer clinic at Carmella College next weekend?" I asked her. "Most of the Kicks are going. You should come and bring as many of your teammates as you can."

Sasha smiled. "That's a fabulous idea. I think just about everyone on the team will want to go. Do you have the info?"

We pulled out our phones, and I sent her the website with the registration information.

"Devin, you are awesome! Thanks so much. You'll definitely see me and most of the other Roses there."

I returned her smile. It felt good to be able to help someone who was in the same situation I'd been in.

Maisie came running back out into the yard. "I'm the monkey! I'm the monkey!"

Sasha looked at me. "Should we go easy on her?"

"No way!" I said, but then I relented. "Well, maybe a little bit."

Sasha hung out with me and Maisie until lunchtime, and then her mom picked her up. Later that afternoon Jessi's face popped up on my phone screen.

"Hey, Dev!" she said. "What's up? I am totally bored. What'd you do today?"

"Not much," I said. I didn't tell her that Sasha had come over, and I wasn't sure why. I guess I didn't think it was newsworthy.

Boy, was I wrong!

# CHAPTER FIVE

"It's nuggets day!" Jessi cheered the next day at lunch. She slid into the seat next to me and put down her lunch tray holding milk, an apple, and a pile of chicken nuggets. "I'm glad Mom gave me lunch money today."

"Lucky!" I said. "I've got turkey rollups again."

"Salad for me," Frida chimed in. "Miriam says to avoid fried foods, but those nuggets look really good."

"Don't get any ideas," Jessi said, putting a protective hand over her plate.

I glanced over at Emma, who hadn't even opened up her bento box.

"What do you have today, Emma?" I asked.

She blinked. "Me? Oh. Vegetable sushi, I think," she replied. "Does anyone know where Zoe is? Is she out sick?"

"No. She was in my Spanish class," Frida replied. "Why, what's up?"

Emma just frowned. Now, it wasn't unusual for one of us to be missing at lunch. Mostly the five of us sat together. But sometimes Frida ate with the drama club, or Jessi sat with Cody.

"Earth to Emma?" Frida asked.

Emma shook her head. "It's nothing. I've just been wanting to talk to her about something, but . . ." She sighed. "There's no point."

"Don't bottle up your feelings like that, Emma!" Jessi said. "If you've got something to say to Zoe, just say it! It's not healthy to keep things inside you. Unless they're nuggets." She popped one into her mouth.

Emma smiled, and then Frida started talking about this old movie she had seen with Miriam, and Emma was fine.

Until practice that afternoon.

"We've all got to remember the pressure that is on our goalies," Coach Flores said at practice. "So we'll all be taking a turn in the goal today."

A lot of the Kicks groaned, but Emma and Zarine, who played goal, both gave shouts of excitement as they high-fived. We had done this drill before, and it was intense.

"Devin, you're up first," Coach Flores said. I sighed. On a great team the players knew what it took to succeed in every position. These kinds of drills made us stronger overall. Yet they weren't easy.

I slipped on the goalie gloves as I headed into the goal,

and braced myself. The Kicks lined up to launch balls at me as fast as they could.

Jessi was first. She grinned as Coach yelled, "Go!" Then Jessi ran up to kick the ball.

It came flying at me, high and fast, and I had to jump up to block it. I had no sooner dealt with that ball than another ball came barreling at me, this one at my feet. I dove for it, but it skidded through my hands and landed firmly in the back of the net.

"Emma, you're my hero," I panted as my turn was over and she took my place.

"I make it look easy, don't I?" She winked as she slid the gloves on.

I felt much more comfortable facing the goal, lining up with the others to take my shot. Emma blocked every ball that came her way, except for one.

After everyone had taken their turn in the goal, we played a short scrimmage. When practice was over, I headed to the locker rooms with the other Kicks, until I remembered I had promised Sasha that I would ask Coach Flores for advice.

I jogged back to the field. Coach Flores was putting soccer balls into a large mesh bag.

"Coach, you got a second?" I asked.

Coach Flores straightened up. "Always for you, Devin. What's up?"

"So, the game on Saturday, with the Roses? I was talking to Sasha from that team, and she's really upset," I explained. "Sasha says her coach is only focused on everyone having fun, not on winning. But the problem is, they are *not* having fun, and they are not winning, either."

Coach Flores gave me a rueful grin. "Sounds familiar, huh? I seem to remember another coach who had the same problem."

"Yep, but now you are the best coach ever!" I assured her. "Sasha wants to talk to her coach about how she's feeling, but she's nervous. I told her I'd ask you for advice."

"I've met Coach Doyle," Coach Flores said. "She's an English teacher at Santa Flora. I know she doesn't know too much about soccer. The only reason she volunteered to coach the team is because there was no one else to do it. Without Coach Doyle, the Roses wouldn't even exist."

"That's what Sasha said," I told her. "That's why she doesn't want to hurt Coach Doyle's feelings by telling her that everyone on the team is unhappy."

Coach Flores nodded. "Actually, I've been meaning to get in touch after Saturday's game. It looks like Coach Doyle could use a little help. I'll reach out to her."

"That would be great!" I said. "What should I tell Sasha?"

"Encourage Sasha to talk to her," Coach Flores replied. "I don't think she'll get upset. I know she wants to do a good job for the team."

I beamed. "Thanks, Coach!" I said, and I felt great, like I had just solved a big problem. I knew Coach would come through!

Coach Flores smiled at me. "It's the least I can do,

Devin. I feel blessed that you felt like you could talk to me about how you were feeling. Now the Kicks are playing great and everyone is having fun—everything I could have hoped for as a coach."

As I walked back to the locker room, I couldn't wipe the smile off my face. I was eager to grab my phone out of the locker so that I could text Sasha and let her know what had happened.

But I couldn't text Sasha right away, because when I walked into the locker room, I found Emma and Zoe squaring off. Emma had her arms crossed defensively in front of her, and Zoe's cheeks were flushed red. Jessi shot me a warning glance, her eyebrows raised.

"Why didn't you sit with us today at lunch?" Emma was asking Zoe.

I looked at Jessi. Emma had apparently taken her advice to talk to Zoe.

Zoe looked down at the locker room floor. "Sometimes you eat with the kids from the Tree Huggers club. Who cares?"

Emma frowned. "Maybe it wouldn't be weird if you were answering my texts, but it's like you're not even talking to me. Are you mad at me or something?"

Zoe shook her head. "No."

Emma snorted. "I'm the one who should be mad, anyway. You totally flaked on the fan club meeting. You didn't even tell me you weren't going to come."

Jessi and I exchanged glances but didn't say anything.

Zoe had tried to tell Emma, but Emma wouldn't—or didn't want to—listen.

"I tried to tell you I've been busy with some other stuff," Zoe said. Now she also crossed her arms protectively. "I've been doing things with my new friends from the art club, and I wanted to eat with them to talk about a project we're going to start. I didn't realize I needed your permission to do that."

*Ouch!* I cringed. Jessi and I once again exchanged looks, and this time both of our eyebrows were practically on the ceiling.

"I thought friends talked about things," Emma shot back. "Not got permission from each other."

"I've gotta go," Zoe replied as she slung her backpack over her shoulder. "My mom is waiting for me in the parking lot."

"Fine. I've got to go too." Emma turned her back toward Zoe as she shoved her practice gear into her gym bag before hurrying out of the locker room.

Zoe grabbed her gear and walked out a few seconds later. Jessi and I just stared at each other, our mouths hanging open. The other Kicks were clearing out, too, but Jessi and I hung back so we could talk about what had just happened.

"Well, that was awkward," Jessi said finally.

"Tell me about it," I said. "Emma and Zoe never argue. What's going on?"

"I don't know," Jessi replied. "But if this keeps up, we're going to have to take sides."

That startled me. "What do you mean?"

"I mean, if they keep arguing like this, we're going to have to figure out which one is right, and then convince the other one that she's wrong," she replied.

"But that's impossible!" I said. "I mean, Emma is partly wrong, but Zoe is definitely acting weird."

Jessi shrugged. "Maybe they'll make up and we won't have to deal with it."

"I hope so," I said, and I meant it. I did not want to have to choose sides in a battle between Emma and Zoe!

# CHAPTER SIX

Although the week had started out with a lot of stress on Monday, it had ended up being pretty quiet. I talked things over with my friend Kara on Friday night. She was my best friend back in Connecticut. I missed her so much, but we video chatted every chance we got.

"So, the whole Emma and Zoe thing is very confusing. They seemed fine after their fight," I said. "We ate lunch all together on Tuesday like nothing had happened. On Wednesday, Zoe ate with the art club. On Thursday, Emma ate with the Tree Huggers, Kentville's environmental group. Then we all ate lunch together today. It was kind of weird. Jessi and I didn't know what to say, and Emma and Zoe didn't bring it up. Luckily, Frida wasn't in the locker room when the fight happened. Otherwise she would have totally made the entire situation more dramatic."

"Hmmmm." Kara seemed lost in thought. "I would be so upset if we had an argument like that. I wouldn't be able to pretend that nothing had happened. I'd have to talk it over with you. I'd totally have a stomachache if I thought you were mad at me."

When Kara got nervous, or upset, her stomach always hurt. I'd known about that ever since the first day when we'd met in kindergarten, when a boy named Dylan had knocked over her block tower. She'd started crying and had said she had a tummy ache and needed to go home. I'd made her laugh with a dinosaur puppet, and we'd been best friends ever since.

"You're right," I told her. "If we had a fight like that, I wouldn't be able to ignore it either. But at least Emma and Zoe are still talking. Maybe that's just the way they handle things."

Kara shrugged. "All friendships are different," she said. "So hey, tell me more about this soccer clinic you're going to tomorrow."

"I'm excited!" I said. "Our game this week is on Sunday, so Coach Flores found this soccer clinic for us. It's being held by the men's and women's soccer teams at Carmella College, and they'll be teaching us some skills and leading us in drills, stuff like that."

"Skills and drills!" Kara said. "Awesome!" Then she yawned. "I know you're three hours behind me, but it's past my bedtime," she said. "Have fun tomorrow."

"Thanks!" I said. "And good luck in your game!"

Kara and I signed off, and even though it was only eight o'clock in California, I started getting ready for bed. I wanted to make the most of the clinic and work on improving my form and technique. It was going to be great!

The next morning I got up as soon as my alarm went off on my phone, and I bounded into the shower. Then I dressed in my practice clothes and went down to the kitchen, where my mom was sitting at the table, reading the newspaper.

"Good morning! I toasted a slice of whole wheat bread for you, and there's a banana and peanut butter on the counter," Mom said before taking a sip of her coffee.

"Yum!" I said. It was one of my favorite breakfasts. I slathered peanut butter onto the toast and then sliced the banana and put the slices on top.

I sat down at the table with my plate. Mom had poured a big glass of orange juice for me.

"Thanks for taking me to the clinic, Mom," I said between bites of toast.

Mom smiled. "I should thank you. Since we both had to be up early today, Mrs. Dukes asked me if I wanted to go with her to the spa. She's treating herself to a massage and a mani-pedi before the baby is born. And I get to tag along for some pampering, too!"

"I guess that's relaxing," I said. "But I'd rather be at the soccer clinic!"

Mom laughed. "That doesn't surprise me, Devin."

Mom dropped me off at the Carmella College athletic field a little before the eight-thirty check-in time. Jessi met me at the gate, and I noticed that most of the other Kicks were milling around the check-in table, including my co-captain, Grace, who smiled and waved.

"Are you ready to rock this soccer clinic?" Jessi asked, bouncing up and down with excitement.

"Let's show them what the Kicks have got!" I said.

After check-in one of the players from the Carmella Cougars instructed us to head onto the field for warm-ups. As we jogged, I glanced around at the other players who had shown up. I didn't see Sasha or anyone else I recognized as being from the Roses.

The Cougars player had us line up and start jumping jacks. Emma and Zoe lined up on my right, and Jessi and Frida stood on my left. I glanced over at Emma and Zoe, and they looked perfectly normal. *I guess their fight is all over with*, I thought.

A minute later Sasha and ten of her teammates ran onto the field and started warming up with everybody else. Sasha waved, and called, "Hi, Devin!"

I waved back as I continued my jumping jacks. I was glad to see that she and some of the other Roses had made it.

After more jumping jacks, some squats, and a jog around the field, another soccer player named A.J. came out to teach us some tactical drills.

Emma nudged me with her elbow. "He's supercute, don't you think?" she whispered.

I shrugged. He was okay, I guess, medium height with curly dark hair and brown eyes. But I was more interested in what he was saying!

"When you do tactical drills, you think ahead about where and when you are going to take your shots," A.J. explained. "You anticipate what the other team is going to do. You make sure you are always using your peripheral vision. And above all, you need to all be on the same page as a team."

We did some passing and receiving drills before A.J. broke us up into teams for a scrimmage. I noticed that the Roses players were quiet, focused, and intent on learning. They definitely seemed to be on the same page!

After the scrimmage, A.J. had us run even more tactical drills. Next we moved on to technical training with a young woman named Elle. We worked on attack, defense, juggling, and more.

"Four!" Jessi yelled as she kicked the ball and launched it over my head. We both started giggling. We were learning a lot but also having fun.

I noticed Sasha working on a defensive passing drill with her teammates. There were no wisecracks or loud laughs. The Roses were concentrating and taking everything in.

Sasha passed the ball to one of the other Roses, slipping it agilely across the defender who was trying to block her.

Her teammate scored, and then I saw them both smile before slapping palms. The soccer clinic seemed like it was helping the Roses a lot!

I felt like I was learning a lot too. After the technical drills were over, we took a water and snack break while we got a lecture about nutrition for athletes.

Frida sat there, nodding her head as if she'd been eating like a health-food fanatic her entire life, not just for the last two weeks.

"Wouldn't you recommend almond milk over cow's milk?" she asked the lecturer.

Jessi nudged me and whispered into my ear, "It wasn't too long ago that she was begging me for some of my hot Cheetos!"

I laughed. Frida never did anything just a little bit. She always dove in completely, and headfirst. So this new attitude about food and nutrition didn't surprise me.

After the lecture two players from the women's team took over—Kim and Julia.

"We're going to do some mini-tournament play," Kim told us. "Line up. We'll be counting off the teams by four."

Grace, the Kicks' co-captain, nudged me. "Let's line up so the Kicks stick together," she said in a low voice, and I nodded. There was some chaos as all of the players got in line, because other girls were trying to do the same thing with their teams.

We quickly grabbed the blue jerseys to slip over our shirts, and we faced the yellow team for fifteen minutes of play. When the round ended, we'd won, 5–2.

Next we faced the red team, which was made up of Sasha and some of the girls from the Roses.

"This oughta be easy," Grace said to me with a grin, but we were in for a surprise.

The chaotic and frenzied Roses had become focused and energized. We had to hustle to stay on top, and we won the match by only one goal. When the game was over, Sasha ran up to me and fist-bumped me.

"This was a great idea, Devin. Thanks," she said. "I feel like we're getting better already!"

"You are," I agreed. "You're doing great!"

Grace was nearby, and I saw her shake her head. Then she walked over to her friend Megan and started whispering. I could tell that Grace was upset. I didn't care. I wanted to focus on the clinic and not get into drama.

After lunch we got to participate in a really fun shooting game before working on more techniques. It was a soccer fanatic's dream day, and I loved every second of it.

As we were getting ready to leave, Sasha came over to me again.

"Devin!" She gave me a hug. "Thank you for all of your help! We had an awesome week of practices. Coach Flores must have given Coach Doyle some tips. We did all new drills, and Coach Doyle said she's going to do everything she can to help get us a win. And it's all thanks to you!"

"No problem!" I said. "I'm glad I could help."

Sasha grinned. "Now you've got to be on your toes the

next time you play us. We are in it and ready to win it!"

"Bring it!" I said. "I always want to play against the best. It makes me a better player. But the Roses will have to make the play-offs if you're going to face us again."

"We're working on it," Sasha said confidently. "Thanks again, and see you later!"

She waved and walked off, and I went to find Jessi because her mom was supposed to be picking us up. I walked past Grace, who was whispering with all the eighth-grade Kicks now and not just Megan. Grace looked right at me so I knew they were talking about me.

Jessi walked over. "Something's up," she said. "You'd better talk to Grace."

I sighed. Grace and I had had some rough times in the past. I'd thought that was all behind us. But it looked like something new was brewing. Honestly, I had no idea what Grace was upset about now—but I was about to find out!

# CHAPTER SEVEN

"Fine. I'll talk to her," I said to Jessi.

"You need backup?" Jessi asked.

"No. You need to look out for your mom," I replied. "If you see her, tell her I'll just be a minute."

"NP," Jessi said, and she darted off.

I moved toward Grace and the eighth graders. Grace was the tallest of the group, and she was both a great player and a cool, calm leader. She was with Megan, her best friend; Jade and Zarine. Zarine and I had played together on the winter team, the Griffons, and we had become pretty friendly.

I don't like confrontation, but I didn't want anything to jeopardize the great season the Kicks were having. So I went on the offensive. (But in a nice way.)

"Grace, I'm wondering if there's a problem?" I asked. "You seem upset about something."

Grace fixed her blue eyes on me. "Yes, I am," she said. "We were wondering why you are helping another team."

"You mean the Roses?" I asked. I knew she had heard Sasha talking to me.

"Yes, the Roses," Grace said. "Did you tell them about this clinic?"

"Well, yeah, but the clinic is open to everybody," I pointed out.

"But they wouldn't have come if you hadn't told them about it," Megan chimed in.

I thought about it. "No, I guess not."

"That's what I mean, Devin. The Roses are our rivals," Grace said. "Why would you help one of our opponents?"

I felt my face getting flushed. Grace was being totally unreasonable!

"Well, first of all, the Roses are in last place right now," I said. "We've already played them, and we won't play them again unless they get to the play-offs, which is unlikely. And second of all, isn't it just, you know, good sportsmanship?"

"That makes sense," Zarine said in a small voice, but Grace didn't take her eyes off me. Her face softened a little, though.

"Listen, Devin, I know you're a nice person," she said, "but maybe you're being *too* nice. Like, aren't you also friends with Jamie of the Rams? After all she did to us?"

Jamie was the captain of the Riverdale Rams. In the fall her team had messed with our equipment and stuff to try to get us to lose, which was a pretty serious thing to do. But I'd gotten to know Jamie on the Griffons, and I'd realized that she wasn't a bad person, just a person who, for complicated reasons, had an intense need to win.

"I wouldn't say we're friends," I answered. "I mean, we're friendly. But what does that have to do with anything?"

Megan made a *humph* noise.

"What?" I asked.

"It's just, I've seen you and Jamie hanging out, and being friendly at the games and stuff," Megan replied.

"So what?" I asked.

"You're our co-captain, Devin," Grace answered for Megan. "Your loyalty should be to the Kicks."

"I *am* loyal to the Kicks!" I protested, my voice rising.

"Then stop helping the Roses," Megan said. "We were in last place once too, remember? And we made it all the way to the finals. The Roses could still do that too."

At that moment Jessi ran up. "Mom says if she doesn't get a chicken taco in five minutes, she's going to freak out. You done?"

"Yes," I said, and I jogged away with Jessi, shaking my head.

"What was that all about?" Jessi asked as we climbed into her mom's car.

"You're not going to believe this," I said, and I told her everything that had happened.

"Seriously?" she replied. "No way. But wait—*did* you help the Roses?"

"Well, Sasha came over the other day when I was drilling with Maisie, and we talked," I admitted. Jessi raised an eyebrow, but I continued. "The Roses were having the same problem with their coach that we had with Coach Flores. So I talked to Coach Flores for them, and she talked to Coach Doyle, and . . ."

"Does Grace know all of this?" Jessi asked.

"No," I replied. "All she knows is that I told them about the clinic."

"Then make sure she doesn't," Jessi said.

"Why? I didn't do anything wrong," I said. Then it hit me. "Do *you* think I did something wrong?"

"No—I mean, not really," Jessi answered. "I think you were just being nice. But maybe it's a tiny bit weird that you're helping another team so much. Even one in last place."

Jessi's mom chimed in from the front seat, and I realized she had been listening the whole time. I also realized that we had come to a stop in front of Taco Barn.

"I think Devin is exhibiting good sportsmanship," Mrs. Dukes said. "Now, I am going inside to get tacos. You two can join me if you want, or you can keep talking."

"She's pretty cranky these days," Jessi whispered to me as we got out of the car and followed her mom. "I think it has something to do with carrying a tiny human around in her belly all the time."

"It has *everything* to do with that!" Mrs. Dukes called back to us.

"Wow, Mom. Does pregnancy make your hearing better too?" Jessi teased.

Her mom sighed. "That might be the only thing it makes better. Now let's get your baby sibling a taco."

A few minutes later the three of us were eating chicken tacos with guac and chips and queso. The food was delicious, but I was feeling pretty down.

"I just don't need tension with the eighth graders again," I said. "It's like A.J. said. We need to be on the same page as a team."

Jessi nodded. "Yeah, that's true," she said. "At least Emma and Zoe aren't fighting anymore. Can you imagine? It would be like a tsunami of Kicks drama."

"No kidding," I agreed, and then my phone beeped with a text from Sasha.

**Good luck on ur game tomorrow! Maybe we can drill again soon?**

I stared at the words, not sure what to reply. I liked Sasha, and I wanted to help her. But could I help her and still be loyal to the Kicks?

"Who was that?" Jessi asked.

"No one," I said, and I put the phone facedown on the table.

# CHAPTER EIGHT

On Sunday morning Mom, Dad, Maisie, and I headed to the Victorton Middle School soccer field. In the fall season we had lost to the Victorton Eagles once, and then beaten them the next time we'd faced them.

Dad parked the minivan, and I stepped out onto the bright, sunny field. When we'd left the house, the temperature had been 87 degrees, and it was only supposed to get hotter. Mom was already fanning herself with her hand.

"Ugh, another heat wave," she complained. "I thought it was always supposed to be a perfect seventy-two degrees in Southern California?"

"It's not that hot," Dad said. "And anyway, would you rather be scraping ice off your car windows every morning for months on end? Isn't this better?"

"Some ice sounds pretty nice right now," she said. "I'm going to go set up my camp chair."

The Victorton soccer field had only one small set of rickety bleachers on the opposing team's side, so most people who came to see the game brought camp chairs with them. Mom's was fancy, with a canvas canopy on top, because she loved the shade.

I jogged out onto the field to meet up with the team. We had twenty girls on the Kicks roster, because Coach didn't cut anyone who wanted to play. Then she subbed out players during the game. But it looked like there was a bunch of girls missing.

"Is everyone late?" I asked Jessi.

She shook her head. "No. Coach says there's some stomach bug going around. Hailey, Brianna, Jade, Gabriela, Taylor, Alandra, and Olivia are all sick and can't play."

My eyes got wide. "All of them?"

Jessi nodded. "Yeah. That leaves us with only, like, three subs," she said.

Hailey, Brianna, and Taylor were some of our strongest offensive players, and Jade was great on defense. But we still had plenty of strong players left.

"We should be fine," I said.

Jessi shrugged. "Let's see."

"Girls, form a circle!" Coach Flores cried. "We're going to try a new drill."

Curious, I jogged into place. I was always excited to learn something new.

"Grace and Devin, I want you in the middle," Coach Flores said.

I walked into the center of the circle, glancing at Grace. She avoided eye contact with me.

Coach kicked a ball to Zoe, and one to Giselle.

"Giselle, you're going to pass the ball to Devin. Devin will pass it to Grace. Grace will pass it to someone else in the circle. While she's doing that, Zoe will pass her ball to Devin, and then we'll keep going," she said.

Emma raised her hand. "Um, could you please explain that again?"

"If you're in the circle and you have the ball, you pass to Devin," Coach said. "Devin will always pass to Grace. And Grace will pass to anyone she wants to in the circle. And then you keep repeating."

"Like singing a song in the round," Frida said.

Coach grinned. "Exactly!" she said. "Let's see you do it."

I was a little confused too, but then I realized that all I had to do was catch each pass sent to me, and then pass to Grace. I turned to Giselle.

"Let's go!" I called out, and Giselle passed the ball to me. It skidded to the left, and I chased after it and sent it to Grace. Then Zoe sent a pass hurtling toward me, a kick that bounced off the grass and went high, so I had to chase after that one too.

That was some drill! It was fun, but hardest for the two people in the middle of the circle. Coach must have had us do it for a full five minutes before she put Jessi and Megan in the middle. I ran to take my place in the circle, bathed in sweat.

"That was intense!" I said to Grace, who was next to me.

Grace didn't say anything. She was obviously giving me the silent treatment. I wanted to scream. Drama and soccer just did not mix!

We finished the drill, and I splashed some water from the cooler onto my face. A few others did the same. I still hadn't cooled off by the time the game started.

The first half of the game was totally frustrating! The Kicks would get the ball into the Eagles midfield, and then the Eagles would get the ball from us and take it into our midfield, and the ball kept going back and forth like that like a volleyball. We couldn't get the ball into goal range, and neither could they.

I'm not sure what the Eagles' problem was, but I think I knew what was wrong with the Kicks—the heat combined with the lack of subs. Frida's curly hair looked like limp noodles, and although she yelled, "I am the sacred guardian of the volcano!" several times, you could hear that her heart wasn't in it.

In the second half Coach subbed in Anjali for Frida, replaced Zoe with Anna, and put Zarine in for Emma on goal. Everyone else had to stay in. Within the first three minutes one of the Eagles got the ball past Giselle, one of our tired defenders, and then kicked it right past Zarine into the net. I noticed that the Eagles player wasn't sweating at all, and I figured that she had spent the whole first half on the bench. Or maybe she was a lizard. I wasn't sure, because even my pink headband was not stopping the sweat from dripping into my eyes.

I knew I had to stop focusing on being hot. Instead I had to focus on getting past the Eagles defense. There had to be a way.

And then I found one. Jessi passed the ball to me, and I stopped it with my chest. Two Eagles immediately ran up to me, so I got rid of it quickly, passing it forward to Grace. Then I ran up to meet Grace as the Eagles swarmed her.

"Grace!" I called. I was wide open.

Grace was dribbling and staring at Megan, who could not shake the Eagles player who was covering her. One of the Eagles covering Grace kicked it away from her, but because I was near, I intercepted it.

Still open, I tore down the field. When I got into goal range, I kicked the ball toward the goal, not thinking about strategy or faking out the goalie—I just wanted that ball to go in.

My heart skipped a beat as the ball struck the goalie's fingertips, but she didn't catch it, and it bounced into the goal right behind her.

I had scored! The game was tied at 1–1, and that was how the game ended—in a tie, because there were no tiebreakers during regular season play, only in the play-offs.

The Kicks and the Eagles lined up and slapped hands, but neither team did it with much energy. Besides being hot, we all knew that a tie game was not much better than losing. You didn't get the agony of defeat, but you didn't get the thrill of victory, either. And a tie would hurt the Kicks' place in the standings.

Coach Flores was her usual cheerful self as we gathered together before she dismissed the team.

"Conditions were tough today, girls, and you all played your best," she said. "You should be proud of that. I'll see you at practice tomorrow."

"Who wants to try out the new ice cream place in Kentville?" Anna called out.

"That sounds good to me!" Emma said. "Can we all meet there?"

As Emma was talking, I saw the eighth-grade girls walking away without answering.

"Looks like it will be a seventh-grade thing," I said.

Mom and Dad dropped me off at Get the Scoop, the new ice cream shop in downtown Kentville. Actually, they had intended to drop me off, but Maisie kept whining, "Why can't I get ice cream too?" So they came in with us, but thankfully they took their orders to go and left me with my Kicks friends. The seven of us sat together—me, Jessi, Emma, Zoe, Frida, Anna, and Sarah. I couldn't help noticing that Emma and Zoe weren't sitting next to each other like they usually did.

"So, what's up with the eighth graders?" Frida wanted to know as we dug into our ice cream.

"Grace is mad at me," I admitted, and then I had to fill the others in on how I had helped the Roses. "I don't know what to do. I like Sasha, and I'd like to hang out with her again, but I don't want to be disloyal to the Kicks."

"I don't think you're being disloyal," Emma said. "You're just trying to help them."

Zoe shrugged. "I don't know," she said. "It is a little weird, but I know you're loyal to the Kicks, Devin."

I sighed. "That's what Jessi said." Jessi nodded in agreement.

"I think they're right," Frida said. "You're always talking about being focused, Devin. You should focus on the Kicks."

"Do whatever you want," Anna chimed in.

"Yeah," Sarah agreed. "Don't worry about Grace. She'll get over it."

I dipped my spoon into my cup of banana ice cream, no closer to an answer than I had been the day before. Then Emma changed the subject.

"I have to get home soon, because tonight is the big night!" she announced.

"What big night?" I asked.

She shook her head. "Seriously, Devin? I've been talking about it all week. It's the Brady McCoy concert!"

I was sure that Emma had been talking about it all week, and I was equally sure that I had tuned her out.

"Mom got two tickets months ago, one for me and one for Zoe," Emma continued. "I could barely sleep last night, I was so excited! And I still need to decide which T-shirt I'm wearing, my *Mall Mania* T-shirt or the one from his first concert tour."

Zoe didn't say anything as she ate her mint chocolate chip ice cream with chocolate sprinkles.

"Anyway, I'm leaning toward the *Mall Mania* shirt because it's sparkly," Emma said, and then she started telling Zoe how she had looked up images of the stage design online for the concert, and she described it in detail. "It starts off with a cityscape of Los Angeles, and lots of lights, and then later in the show the whole stage looks like a snow mountain peak because Brady loves to ski. . . ."

Zoe didn't say another word the whole rest of the time.

My dad picked up both me and Jessi so that we could bring her home, and I finally got a chance to talk to Jessi about it.

"What do you think is up between Emma and Zoe?" I asked. "It's like they're not fighting, but they're not talking to each other either. It's pretty obvious that Zoe doesn't want to go to that concert. Why doesn't she just say so?"

"I know. It's weird," Jessi agreed. "But I'm not sure how to help them."

"Me neither," I said. "I just hope they can work it out."

"I bet they will," Jessi said.

My phone beeped with another text from Sasha.

**U there?**

I went with my gut. **Yeah, what's up?**

Helping Sasha felt right. Freezing out Sasha didn't. If Grace and the other eighth graders had a problem with that, I would deal with it.

We beat the Panthers today! 😊 ⚽ ⚽ 😊 Sasha texted me.

"The Roses beat the Panthers today!" I told Jessi, the shock evident in my voice.

The Pinewood Panthers were one of the best teams in our division. They had beaten the Kicks once last fall. It was hard to believe that the Roses had turned things around so quickly, but I guess they had. And maybe the heat and the stomach bug going around had hurt the Panthers, too.

Jessi's eyes grew wide. "Wow. Seriously? That's hard to believe."

"That's what Sasha just texted," I said.

Congrats! I replied.

We're coming for you! Sasha texted back, and I knew she was teasing. But I also knew that Grace would not have taken it that way.

Good luck! I replied, and that was the end of our chat.

I sighed with relief. Sasha hadn't asked me for any more help, so my problem with the eighth graders was solved for now.

# CHAPTER NINE

"We have to go back to that ice cream place again," Jessi remarked as we walked to our lunch table the next day in school. "I am obsessed with their salted caramel swirl."

I made a face. "Not a fan of the salty ice cream," I said. "But the banana was awesome."

We sat down and were unpacking our lunches when Emma walked up. Actually, she stomped up, with an angry look on her face. She slammed her lunchbox onto the table.

"Emma, what is wrong?" I asked.

"Zoe," she replied. "I am so mad at her!"

Just then Zoe approached, and Emma glared at her. Zoe put her head down and started to walk to a different table. Emma ran up to her and blocked her path.

"Where were you last night?" Emma asked. "You said your sister Jayne was dropping you off at the concert. But you never showed up!"

Zoe had three older sisters: Jayne, Yvette, and Opal. Jayne had her own car and drove Zoe around sometimes.

"I tried to tell you I didn't want to go, but you wouldn't listen," Zoe protested.

"But you were excited when my mom got us the tickets!" Emma countered.

Emma was talking really loudly, and some of the kids sitting nearby had stopped talking to listen.

"That was months ago," Zoe said. "I don't care about him anymore. I told you that."

Emma folded her arms across her chest. "So where did you go? When I called your house looking for you, your mom thought you were with me."

"That's exactly why *I* should be mad at *you*," Zoe said. "My mom freaked out when you called. Now I'm grounded for a month!"

"You still haven't told me where you went," Emma said.

"That's none of your business," Zoe replied.

Emma's face turned red. "None of my business?" Her voice was a shrill shriek.

Jessi jumped up. "Time to intervene," she said, and I followed her lead. She walked up to Zoe and pulled her away, and I grabbed Emma by the arm and pulled her back to the table.

"I can't believe her!" Emma said. "We're supposed to be best friends, and she ditches me. And when I ask her why, she says it's none of my business."

"Yeah, that's rough," I agreed.

Emma looked at me. "So you're on my side, then, Devin? You know I'm right."

I panicked. I didn't know what to say to Emma, because I thought Zoe had a point too. She'd been trying to tell Emma for a while now that she wasn't into Brady McCoy. I'd heard her start many times.

"Well . . . ," I began, but then I was interrupted by a tap on my shoulder. I turned to see Grace and Megan.

"Devin, did you know that the Roses beat the Panthers yesterday?" Grace asked.

I felt my face flush. "Well . . ." That was becoming my favorite word.

"We thought so," Megan said. "Thanks a lot."

"Thanks for what?" I asked. "It's not like I was on the field with them!"

But they both turned and walked away without another word. I sat down and put my face in my hands, groaning.

"Is that about the Sasha thing?" Emma asked, but right then Jessi came back and slid into her seat.

"Okay, so I found out where Zoe was last night," Jessi said.

"Nice. She tells you, but she won't tell me," Emma said.

Jessi ignored her. "So, she went to a concert with some kids from the art club." She nodded over to Zoe and the table she was sitting at, with some of the art club kids. I recognized Jasmine, a girl with a dark pink streak in her brown hair, and Arthur, a quiet boy who always wore all black.

When I turned back to our table, I saw that Frida had her phone pointed at me, and I realized she had been quiet this whole time.

"What are you doing?" I asked.

"This lunch period is a jackpot of emotions," she replied. "I'm recording everyone's facial expressions so that I can practice them. You guys have been doing some great ones. Anger, surprise, disbelief, rejection, fear . . ."

Jessi answered Frida with a look—a look that told her to put the phone down, and Frida did.

"What concert could be better than a Brady McCoy concert?" Emma wondered.

"A concert at a small all-ages club in Victorton," Jessi replied. "For some band I've never heard of."

"I still don't get it," Emma said. "Why didn't she tell her mom where she was going? Why did she lie and say she was with me?"

"No idea," Jessi said.

"Unless maybe her mom didn't want her to go to an all-ages club in Victorton," I guessed. I knew my mom wouldn't. Usually teenagers and college kids went to those clubs.

"Well, whatever the reason, now she's in big trouble," Jessi said.

"Poor Zoe," Frida said.

"Ha! Are you kidding?" Emma blurted out. "She disappointed me, and she lied to her mom. She deserves to be in big trouble. I thought *you* would understand that, Frida."

Frida held up both her hands. "All right, calm down. But there's two sides to every story, you know."

"There is only one side to this story, and it's my side," Emma said stubbornly.

I felt a knot forming in my stomach. I did not want to have to choose between Emma and Zoe. I did not want to have to choose between helping Sasha and staying friendly with Grace. I felt stuck in the middle of everything, and it wasn't a good place to be.

Then Jessi brilliantly changed the subject.

"Emma, what's in your lunchbox today? Did your mom pack those spicy noodles again?" she asked.

"Yeah, I think so," Emma replied. "And the cucumber salad."

Jessi held up a banana and wiggled it. "Maybe we can work out a trade."

"For a banana? Are you kidding?" Emma asked, and then we were all joking and laughing and everything was back to normal. Except that Emma and Zoe weren't speaking to each other, and Grace was still mad. Ugh!

# CHAPTER TEN

Soccer practice that afternoon started off badly and just got worse.

"We're going to learn a new drill today," Coach Flores told us after we had warmed up. "It's a little complicated but it's fun, and I think it will improve our shooting and passing. Follow me out onto the field, and I'll show you."

Coach Flores jogged onto the field, and we followed her. I saw Grace and Megan roll their eyes.

"You gonna share this drill with the Roses, Devin?" Grace asked me.

I sighed. "Come on. It's not like that!"

But they ignored me and jogged ahead. I looked at Jessi next to me, who had heard the whole thing.

"I do not understand what they are so upset about," I said.

Jessi shrugged. "I'm sure it will blow over."

I was happy to see Hailey, Brianna, Taylor and Olivia there. At least they didn't seem mad at me!

"Are you feeling better?" I asked them.

Hailey nodded. "It was one of those twenty-four hour things. I feel fine again, but my mom has it now. She is miserable!"

Olivia said, "Jade, Gabriela and Alandra are still feeling awful. They weren't in school today."

Jessi covered her mouth and nose with her hands. "I don't want to catch it!"

"If you haven't yet, you're probably safe," Hailey told her.

Coach had set up four cones in a square—two cones ten feet apart on the edge of the penalty box in front of the goal, and two more cones ten feet behind them. She had Zoe, Emma, Taylor, and Anjali stand by the four cones. Emma stood by the cone on the left side closest to the goal, and Anjali stood by the right cone closest to the goal. Taylor stood by the cone diagonally across from Anjali, and Zoe stood by the cone diagonally across from Emma.

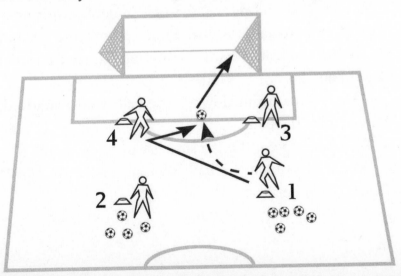

"Seventh graders, line up behind Zoe," Coach instructed. "Eight graders, line up behind Taylor."

I lined up behind Zoe with Jessi, Frida, Brianna, Hailey, Anna, Sarah, and Olivia.

"This is a diagonal drill," Coach explained. "Zoe is in position number one, so she will go first. She's going to pass the ball diagonally to Emma, who's in position number four." Coach walked from Zoe to Emma, demonstrating.

"Then Zoe will run forward, and Emma will pass it to her, and Zoe will kick it into the goal," Coach went on. "Zoe moves to position four, Emma retrieves the ball and passes it to Taylor in position two. Then Emma moves to the back of the eighth grade line and Taylor passes the ball diagonally to Anjali. And then we keep going. Got it?"

Believe it or not, we did get it. It might have sounded confusing, but it was easy to figure out when Coach demonstrated on the field.

"All right, Zoe. Let's begin," Coach said.

Zoe nodded and passed the ball smoothly to Emma. Then Zoe ran toward the goal. Emma passed it to her, but she kicked the ball so hard that it whizzed past Zoe and out of bounds.

"Jeez, Emma, calm down!" Zoe called out, annoyed, chasing after the ball.

"You calm down!" Emma shot back.

"Zoe, just dribble the ball back and make the goal!" Coach called out.

Zoe obeyed, and then she and Emma crossed paths as Zoe took Emma's place by the cone. I saw Zoe say something to Emma, but I couldn't hear it. Then Emma scowled and stomped all the way to the back of the eighth-grade line.

I looked at Jessi and raised my eyebrows.

"This is not good," I whispered.

"No, it isn't," Jessi agreed.

The drill continued, and even though some of us were confused about where to go or where to pass the ball, we quickly got the hang of it after a few rounds. We kept going until everybody had had a chance in all four positions. At one point Zoe had to pass the ball to Emma again. She aimed a precise, perfect pass that rolled right in front of Emma's feet.

"That's how you do it," Zoe said, loud enough for Emma to hear. Emma glared at her and kicked the ball into the goal so hard that it bounced off the net and flew back onto the field. Zoe chased after it, shaking her head.

When we finished the drill, Coach split us up for a scrimmage.

"Let's do seventh grade versus eighth grade, just for fun," she said.

"Oh boy," I muttered under my breath. Of all the times for Coach Flores to split us up by grade, I had a feeling this was not a good idea. And I was right.

Grace and the eighth graders got into a huddle before the scrimmage started, and when they came out of it, they were super high-energy, which turned into their becoming totally aggro on the field. They were on top of the ball like peanut butter on jelly. I could barely get near it.

It didn't help that Emma and Zoe took their argument onto the field. Emma stopped a goal by Giselle, and Zoe was clear for a pass, but Emma passed it to Hailey, who was guarded by two eighth graders, Jade and Taylor.

"Emma, I was free!" Zoe yelled.

"Don't tell me how to play!" Emma yelled back, and while she was distracted, Jade sent a ball whizzing past her ear into the net.

The seventh graders lost the scrimmage 4–0, and Grace and the eighth graders looked pretty pleased with themselves. Coach Flores, on the other hand, sensed that something was up.

"Good job, eighth grade," she said. "I love the energy you had on the field. I'd love to see you use that against the Tigers on Saturday."

Grace and Megan high-fived.

Then Coach turned to me and my team. "Seventh grade, you guys were not as focused as you should be," she said, looking right at Emma and Zoe. "We all need to work together as a team if we're going to succeed."

She looked back at the eighth graders now. "All of us."

"Yes, Coach!" we all said, and I hoped that everyone meant it.

When I got home from practice, I showered and then had a video chat with Kara before dinner. When her face popped up on the screen, I saw that she was sitting at her kitchen table with piles of papers around her.

"Bad time?" I asked her.

"It's okay," she said with a yawn. "I've been studying for my science test for the past two hours. I could use a break! How was practice?"

"Full of drama," I replied, and then I told her everything that had happened. Kara's eyes got wide.

"So I guess things aren't any better with Zoe and Emma?" she asked.

"No, and I don't know how to fix it," I said.

Kara frowned thoughtfully. "Maybe you can't fix it, Devin. Maybe this is something the two of them have to work out for themselves."

"Maybe," I said. "But you know me. I like to fix things."

Kara laughed. "Yeah, I remember last year when Aimee and Alexis got into that big fight, and you held, like, a court proceeding at the cafeteria table."

I laughed. "I hate drama! And things usually get better when you talk them out."

"Well, Aimee stormed away from the table, remember?" Kara asked.

"Yes, but she and Alexis made up the next day," I pointed out. "And I think it's because I put the idea into their heads. Broke the ice."

"Hmm. Good point," Kara said. "Maybe you need to break the ice somehow with Emma and Zoe."

I sighed. "Maybe. If I can get them into the same

room. Zoe hasn't been sitting with us recently."

"Wow," Kara said. "And that's not your only problem. I do not understand what is up with Grace. She is making a big deal out of nothing."

"I know!" I agreed. "And now it's affecting the team. And that is not good."

"Not good at all," Kara agreed. "But if anyone can bring the team back together, it's you, Devin."

I suddenly felt really sad that Kara was three thousand miles away and not right next to me.

"I miss you so much!" I blurted out.

"Miss you too!" Kara said. She leaned forward and kissed the camera, and I laughed.

"Maybe Emma and Zoe just need to live across the country from each other," Kara said. "You and I never fight!"

"True," I said, "but there's got to be a simpler way."

I said good night to Kara and headed downstairs to dinner, the wheels turning in my head. I knew they wouldn't stop turning until all of this drama was over!

# CHAPTER ELEVEN

My eyes went wide when I saw the food that Jessi was pulling out of her lunch bag the next day in the cafeteria. A container of perfectly shaped tiny globes of cantaloupe and honeydew melon. A green salad with artfully rolled-up salami and cheese, and radishes cut to look like flowers. A tiny container of dressing.

"Fancy," Frida said. "Did Emma's mom pack your lunch?"

Jessi shook her head. "No. Mom's been feeling all guilty because I'm going to feel ignored when the new baby comes, so she stayed up late last night making this. There's even a tiny ice pack in here to keep it all fresh."

"Wow!" I said, peeling the lid off my yogurt cup.

"And there's a note," Jessi said. She pulled out a piece of pale purple paper. "Mom wrote me a poem, like those poems we learned how to write in English. Where you take a word, and each letter in the word begins a line of the poem."

The name for that popped into my head. "An acrostic," I said.

Jessi nodded. "Yup." She read the poem and started shaking her head. "Oh gosh. She's gone off the deep end. '*J* is for the joy you bring me. *E* is for every day you've been in my life.'"

"That's so sweet!" Frida said.

"I guess," Jessi replied. "She's just so emotional lately! Dad says it's the pregnancy hormones. I guess maybe I'll be glad when this baby finally comes."

She took a bite of her salad. "Mmm. This is almost as good as what Emma's mom would pack," she said, and then she looked around. "Where is Emma, anyway?"

I glanced around the crowded cafeteria and saw Emma sitting with her friends from the Tree Huggers.

"Tree hugging," I replied. "Well, not literally, but you know what I mean."

"I guess it's just the three of us, then," Frida said. "Have the fabulous five broken up?"

"First of all, when did we ever call ourselves the fabulous five?" Jessi asked. "Secondly, nobody's breaking up. Look, here comes Zoe."

Zoe walked over to our table carrying a lunch tray. I noticed that she had a blue streak in her blond hair.

"Hey," she said, sitting down as though she hadn't stopped sitting with us for the last week.

"Zoe, your hair looks amazing!" Frida said.

"Kicks blue!" I added.

Zoe shrugged. "Yvette did it for me last night," she said. "It is so boring being grounded. But I can thank Emma for that."

Jessi and I looked at each other. It sounded like Zoe was about to get into it.

"So, your mom was pretty mad at you, huh?" Jessi asked. "For going to that concert?"

"She never would have known about it if Emma hadn't called her," Zoe said.

I couldn't keep my thoughts to myself any longer. "But it's not like Emma called your mom on purpose. She honestly thought you were supposed to be at the Brady McCoy concert with her, and she was worried about you."

Zoe's blue eyes flashed. "I tried to tell Emma a million times that I wasn't going to that dumb concert! But she wouldn't listen!"

Frida nodded. "That's true."

"See? Frida's taking my side," Zoe said.

"Well, actually—" Frida began, but Zoe interrupted her.

"What about you, Devin and Jessi?" Zoe asked. "Whose side are you on? Because it seems like you're on Emma's side in all of this."

"Listen, it's not fair to ask us to take sides," Jessi said bluntly. "Emma should have listened to you. But it's your own fault that you went to that concert without telling your mom."

"Because I *couldn't* tell my mom. Don't you get it?" Zoe shot back. "She's getting all freaked out about me hanging out with Jasmine and Arthur. She says they're a bad influence, which is so dumb. Just because their parents let them go to all-ages clubs and take the bus by themselves to places where interesting things happen."

I thought about my own mom, who I knew wouldn't let me go to all-ages clubs or take the bus with my friends either. Then I remembered something. "Jasmine has a pink streak in her hair, right? Did your mom let you put the blue in?"

Zoe grimaced. "I didn't ask her. She grounded me for an extra week."

"That stinks," Jessi said. "I'm sorry."

"Then you get it," Zoe said. "So that means you're definitely on my side, right?"

"Zoe, we can't choose between the two of you," I said. "Like Jessi said, it's just not fair. We love you both."

"This is not about love," Zoe said firmly. "It's about what's right and what's wrong."

"How Shakespearean!" Frida chimed in.

"Can't you and Emma just talk it out?" I suggested, remembering Kara's advice. "You guys have been friends forever."

"Well, things change," Zoe said darkly. "People change."

Then she got up and walked over to Jasmine and Arthur and sat with them.

"Well, that certainly was a dramatic exit," Frida remarked.

"This has to stop," Jessi said. "Like, now."

"Yeah, but what can we do?" I asked. "Maybe we should wait and let them work it out."

"Or maybe we should help them," Jessi said. "Because as my mom's poem states, 'S is for your seriousness about your friends and family.'"

"Wow, she's a pretty bad poet," Frida said.

"Definitely," Jessi said. "But she's right. I am very serious about my friends. If Zoe and Emma won't work this out, we'll make them work it out."

I had no idea what Jessi had in mind, but I was glad that she was taking charge of the situation. I just hoped that she could make her plan happen before things got out of control!

# CHAPTER TWELVE

"Go, Kicks!"

At our Saturday morning game against the Newton Tigers, the stands were packed with fans wearing blue. We always got a bigger turnout on our home field, and the temperature had returned to a reasonable 75 degrees, with blue skies overhead.

We were on the field, doing a shooting drill before the game started. I stood in line behind Zarine, waiting for my turn to shoot.

While we waited, Zarine turned and nodded toward the other end of the field, where the Tigers were warming up. They looked like tigers in their white, orange, and black uniforms.

"See that girl?" Zarine asked.

"Which one?" I replied.

I shaded my eyes with my hand to get a better look,

not sure what Zarine meant. And then I spotted her.

A girl with bright red hair was zooming around the field, dribbling the ball as she went. Her ponytail bounced against her neck. She wasn't just fast—she was *fast*.

"That's Kathy Finnegan," Zarine explained. "She just transferred to Newton from New York a few months ago. She's so fast that they call her the Flying Finnegan."

"Wow," I said. "I can see that."

"This should be an interesting game," Zarine went on. "The Tigers beat us in the fall. And now they've got a secret weapon."

"Well, not so secret," I said. "But, yeah, it will be interesting."

Suddenly I realized that Zarine and I were having a normal conversation—and she was an eighth grader. She didn't seem mad at me at all. Maybe she could help me straighten out the whole thing with Grace.

"Zarine, I need to ask you something," I began, but then Coach called out to us and I couldn't finish.

I ran onto the field and took my position as forward along with Hailey, who smiled at me, and Grace, who didn't even look at me. When the game started, the Tigers got control of the ball. One of the players passed it to the Flying Finnegan—and she charged down the field like a rocket.

I ran as fast as I could, but I couldn't catch up to her. Our midfielders couldn't catch up to her either. And she blew past our defenders to then make a shot at the goal.

Emma was on goal, and she jumped up high as the ball soared above her. She batted it away with two hands. It was a magnificent save, but I knew that Emma was going to need to make a lot more of those before the game was over.

And I was right. The Tigers' strategy seemed to be to pass the ball to Kathy Finnegan and let her run for the goal. Emma stopped three more goals, but then one landed in the net. Coach switched out Emma for Zarine halfway through the first half, but that made total sense; any goalie going up against the Flying Finnegan was going to need a rest!

While our defense couldn't stop the Flying Finnegan, our offense couldn't score. Part of the problem was that Grace wouldn't pass to me, and I knew she was doing it on purpose. There were plenty of times when she could have, and she either passed to Hailey or kept plowing through the Tigers defense, who kept taking the ball from her.

So I was relieved when the second half started and Coach replaced us with Megan and Brianna. The two of them worked well together on the field, and each of them scored pretty quickly. So with six minutes left to go, the score was Kicks 2, Tigers 1.

Sitting on the bench, I realized that one of the problems with the Flying Finnegan strategy was that while Kathy Finnegan was fast, her goal shots were what I would describe as messy. She just kicked it when she got close, without really setting up or strategizing the shot. So a few of her shots just missed, and a lot of them were kicked directly into Emma's or Zarine's waiting arms.

Even so, I still admired the Flying Finnegan. Because the idea that I might someday go pro had been implanted in my brain, like a seed, and I knew that if I wanted to go pro, I had to be fast too. As fast as Kathy Finnegan, if not faster.

The Flying Finnegan scored again, tying up the game 2–2. Coach Flores called Megan and Hailey out and put in me and Jessi as forwards along with Brianna.

The three of us had a lot of energy, and we stayed focused on getting to that goal. First Jessi passed the ball to me, and I passed to Brianna, but the pass got intercepted by one of the Tigers and ended up with the Flying Finnegan. This time she didn't get to make her shot.

"Be gone, foul speed demon!" Frida cried, running up to the Flying Finnegan faster than I'd ever seen her run. She kicked the ball away from Kathy, and Zoe got it. Zoe brought the ball up to the midfield and then passed it to Brianna. Jessi and I chased after Brianna as she dribbled to the Tigers' goal.

Two Tigers caught up to Brianna, so she passed the ball to me. When I had a clear shot, I aimed for the left corner of the goal. The goalie dove for it, but it whizzed past her. The score was Kicks 3, Tigers 2, and the game ended a minute later.

"Yay, Kicks!" The fans in the Kentville stands went wild, cheering for us. We lined up on the field to shake hands with the Tigers, and when Grace jogged past me, she actually smiled at me!

"We're all going for frozen yogurt!" Grace announced when we were gathered around Coach Flores. I grinned at Jessi. Grace had said "all." The team was back together again!

Soon we were sitting at three picnic tables outside the yogurt shop. I was digging into a cup of banana yogurt with chocolate chips, because I was starting to become obsessed with that combination. Frida was explaining how she had channeled enough speed to catch up to the Flying Finnegan.

"I had to reach down deep into my soul," she said. "I imagined that I was a cheetah, racing across the savanna."

"I'm sure the fact that you've been hitting the gym regularly has something to do with it too," Jessi said.

Frida nodded. "It was a mind, body, and spirit experience, for sure."

"Well, I'm glad you did," Emma said. "Fending off goals from that girl was exhausting!"

"They call her the Flying Finnegan," I reported. "Zarine told me."

"Well, even with the Flying Finnegan, the Tigers couldn't beat us," Jessi said. She held up her yogurt cup. "Cheers!"

Everyone at our table clinked yogurt cups. I glanced over at the table next to us, where Zoe was sitting with some of the other seventh graders. I caught her looking at us, and then she looked away.

I frowned, and then whispered to Jessi, "Well, we may be closer to solving the eighth-grade problem, but our Zoe-Emma problem is only getting worse."

As I was saying this, a bunch of girls in Roses jerseys walked up to the yogurt shop. I waved at Sasha, who waved back. Then two of the girls stopped in front of the Kicks tables. They looked older, like they might be eighth graders.

"Look, it's the *Kicks*," said one of the girls, with straight, sun-streaked brown hair.

"We'll see *you* in the play-offs," said the other girl, whose black hair was pulled back into a short ponytail.

"You've got to win some games to get to the play-offs, Ashley," Grace said, and then she and the girls at her table started laughing.

The girl with sun-streaked hair glared at Grace. "Oh, we're winning, Gross—I mean, *Grace*," she said, and the girl next to her giggled. "We won again today. And if you make it to the play-offs with us, we'll win again."

The two Roses girls walked away.

Grace got up from the table and stomped over to me. "Are you happy now, Devin?" she asked, and then she walked away from the yogurt shop and sat on a bench down the street, fuming. Megan got up and ran after her.

"I guess that eighth-grade problem is still on," Jessi remarked.

"Yeah," I agreed, but something was bugging me. I had a feeling that this whole thing was about more than just me helping Sasha.

I got up and approached Zarine at her table. "Can I talk to you for a sec?" I asked.

Zarine nodded. "Sure," she said, and she followed me a few feet away, to where we could talk.

"I'm just wondering if something is up between Grace and that girl from the Roses," I said.

"Ashley," Zarine replied. "She's captain, and the girl with her was Kinsley, her co-captain. Ashley and Grace got into it back in soccer camp this summer. They met, and it was like fire and ice. Or oil and water, or something like that. They just can't get along and are supercompetitive with each other. So Grace took it personally when you started helping Ashley's team."

That made perfect sense. "But I didn't go to soccer camp this summer! I had no way of knowing. Why didn't she just tell me?"

Zarine shrugged. "I don't know. That's Grace, I guess."

"Is there anything I can do?" I asked. "I hate that she's so mad at me about this."

"Keep winning games," Zarine said. "And stop helping the Roses. Once Grace sees that, she'll come around."

"Um, sure," I said. I understood the "winning games" part, but I wasn't sure how I felt about the "stop helping the Roses" part. That was my decision, not Grace's, right?

Zarine sat down, and as I walked back to my table, Sasha and some Roses came out of the shop carrying their yogurts.

"Hey, Devin!" Sasha called out cheerfully.

I nodded. "Hey," I said, smiling back at her. "See you around."

I still wasn't sure if I was going to keep helping the Roses with advice. But I was still going to be nice to Sasha, no matter what Grace said!

"What did Zarine say?" Jessi asked me, and as I started to explain, in a low voice, Grace and Megan came back. They sat back down at their table, and Grace motioned for the other girls to lean in. They started whispering.

"That's weird," Jessi remarked.

"Yeah," I agreed, and I had a funny feeling in my stomach. I finished my banana yogurt with chocolate chips, Frida started doing her impression of a British whale (which is a lot funnier than it sounds), and the sun was shining—and for a while I could enjoy the fact that we had faced the Flying Finnegan and won!

# CHAPTER THIRTEEN

The temperature soared back into the eighties the week after the Tigers came, but there was a definite chill in the air. Emma and Zoe were not speaking at all. And Grace and Megan and most of the eighth graders were still not speaking to me.

At lunchtime Zoe sat with her art friends almost all the time, and Emma took turns sitting with us or the Tree Huggers. So on Thursday it was just me, Jessi, and Frida at our lunch table.

"I cannot take being frozen out by everyone anymore," I complained. "This has gone too far. We need to resolve things before Saturday's game."

"So, how can we solve the problem?" Frida asked.

"I'm sure if Emma and Zoe just talked to each other, they could work out their problems," I replied. "But we can't even get them into the same room. Kara thinks that if we could get them together, they might talk things out."

"Leave that to me," Jessi said, and she started scrolling through her phone. "What are you guys doing tomorrow night, after practice? Like at around seven?"

"I'm free," I replied.

Frida picked up her phone. "Let me check my schedule," she said. "Hmm. I was supposed to do a half hour in front of the mirror practicing my facial expressions, but I can move that."

"Are you still doing that?" Jessi asked.

"Of course," Frida said. "Try me."

"Um, sad," Jessi said.

"That's easy," Frida replied, and she frowned slightly, lowering her eyelids.

"Awesome!" Jessi cheered. "You pick one, Devin."

"Um, how about frustrated?" I suggested. "As in, frustrated because your two friends aren't talking to each other and you don't know how to help them?"

"No problem," Frida said, and this time her eyes narrowed and her frown became crooked, and she looked exactly as I was feeling.

"Well, practice your expression for surprised, because that's how you're going to feel tomorrow night when you see what I've done," Jessi said. "Just leave it to me."

"I am happy to," I said. "Do you have any ideas about what to do about the eighth graders? I caught them whispering again at practice last night. It's got me worried."

"I'll find out what they're up to," Frida promised. "I

haven't gotten into spy mode in a while. It should be fun."

"So don't worry, Devin," Jessi said. "We got this. Frida, show Devin your chill face."

Frida made what I can only describe as a "super-chill" expression, and I smiled. With Jessi and Frida-the-spy on the case, I had a feeling that things might just get better after all.

After practice on Friday, I showered at home, and then we ate some Chinese take-out food from Panda House, which is a rare occasion at our house. Mom let us order only steamed chicken and vegetables with sauce on the side, but I didn't mind, because it was really delicious no matter how much sauce you put on it. And Dad always snuck in an order of egg rolls for all of us.

When dinner was over, Dad dropped me off at Jessi's house. Jessi answered the door when I rang the bell.

"Good. You're here," she said. "Frida texted that she's going to be late. But Zoe and Emma should be here any minute."

"How did you get them to agree to come here?" I asked.

Jessi just grinned at me, and the doorbell rang. It was Zoe.

"You didn't say Devin was going to be here," Zoe blurted out when Jessi opened the door. "I mean, that's cool, but Emma's not here, right?"

"No, Emma's not here," Jessi said truthfully. "Why don't you guys head to my room? I'll be right there."

"Sure," Zoe said with a shrug, and I followed her. I had a feeling I knew what was going to happen next.

Jessi's bedroom was small but cozy, with a string of tiny blue and white lights draped along the blue walls. It used to be her father's office, and Jessi's bedroom used to be upstairs. But her parents needed that room for the baby, so Jessi had been kicked out.

"This is such a cute space," Zoe said, flopping down onto the bed. "I've got to share my room with Opal for a few more years."

"I am so glad I don't have to share with Maisie," I said. "I think I'd go crazy."

Zoe grinned. "Crazy with Maisie!" she said, but then the doorbell rang again and her smile faded. "Who's that? Frida? When Jessi invited me over, she said it would be just the two of us. She said she wanted someone to watch *House of Screams* with her because she was too scared to watch it alone."

I shrugged. I didn't know what to say. Jessi had obviously woven a large web of deception, and I didn't want to ruin any of it.

Then Jessi walked into the room with Emma.

Zoe sat up. "What is *she* doing here?"

"What are *you* doing here?" Emma shot back. She turned to Jessi. "You told me you wanted me to come over to watch the *Pony Pals* movie with you because Devin thought it was too silly. Was that a lie?"

"Yes!" Jessi said, closing the door behind her. "But I had to do it. You two won't listen to reason."

"I am being very reasonable," Zoe snapped. "Emma is the one not listening."

"Are you kidding?" Emma asked. "How can I listen when you won't talk to me?"

"You're not talking to me either," Zoe shot back.

"You're the one who stopped sitting with us at lunch first!" Emma argued. "And how many times did I text you? Like, a million! And you didn't reply!"

Jessi held up her arms. "All right, guys. Calm down!" she said. "I didn't bring you here to fight."

Zoe jumped off the bed. "No, you brought me here under false pretenses. I'm leaving."

"Please!" I blurted out. "Please just stay, Zoe. I don't know what Jessi has planned. Let's find out."

Zoe stopped.

"You guys don't have to talk to each other if you don't want to," Jessi said. "I just need you to watch."

"Watch what? *Pony Pals*?" Emma asked.

"No. This is much better," Jessi said. She walked over to her laptop, which was propped up on some books on her desk. Then she pressed a button, and the screen came to life.

On the screen was the title *Emma and Zoe: Friends Through the Ages*.

"Seriously?" Zoe muttered under her breath.

Music started playing, and a slideshow began. The first slide was a class picture of a bunch of really little kids.

"Kindergarten!" Emma cried. "Where we all met!"

The next picture showed three little girls in costumes. Emma was a witch, Zoe was a superhero, and Jessi was a cute little puppy dog.

"Awwwww!" I couldn't help myself. "You guys are so cute!"

"Remember that day?" Jessi asked. "Emma got scared by a mechanical ghost that came to life at somebody's house, and Zoe gave Emma her candy to make her feel better."

"That was really sweet of you," Emma said, with a glance at Zoe. Zoe didn't smile, but she settled back in on the bed.

More pictures popped up. Emma and Zoe in their first soccer uniforms. Jessi blowing out birthday candles with Emma and Zoe on either side of her. The three of them at a school fair. The girls got older in each picture, and it reminded me that my California friends had all known one another for a long time before I'd moved here. Except for Frida. They had met her in middle school.

So it made me happy when I finally started appearing in the pictures, and Frida, too. There we all were, eating pizza after one of our fall games. And then there was a photo of us all dressed up for Zoe's bat mitzvah.

Then words came up on the screen. *Friends 4Ever . . . Right?*

The music stopped, and the words stayed on the screen. Nobody said anything for a few seconds.

"I hate fighting with you, Zoe," Emma said. "I love you. And I do always want to be your friend."

"Me too," Zoe said, but she still wasn't looking at Emma. "But, Em, you need to understand. I'm just not into Brady

McCoy anymore. You know, we're getting older, and that means that we won't always like the same things."

Emma nodded. "Yeah, I figured that out," she said. "But that doesn't mean we can't be friends, does it?"

"No," Zoe replied. "But it might mean, like, we don't always do things together. Like maybe sometimes I'll do things with Jasmine and Arthur."

"Things I'm not invited to?" Emma asked.

"Well . . ." Zoe looked thoughtful. "I mean, I can invite you to stuff. And you can say no if you're not into it. And the same goes for me. Does that make sense?"

Emma nodded. "Yeah, I understand."

"This is truly beautiful," Jessi said. "Now hug it out!"

Emma and Zoe hugged, and a wave of relief washed over me. Then the doorbell rang. We heard Mrs. Dukes answer it, and then running feet. Frida burst into Jessi's room.

"Sorry I'm late, but I have big news!" she announced. "My spying was successful!"

Emma and Zoe looked puzzled, so I filled them in. "Frida was going to find out what the eighth graders have been whispering about."

Frida nodded. "I went undercover," she said.

"As an eighth grader?" I asked. "How would that work, exactly?"

"No. I mean, I was myself, but I pretended that I didn't like you, Devin," Frida answered.

I cringed. "Oh."

"I walked home with Gabriela and Jade after practice," Frida explained, "and I told them I thought you were a traitor for helping the Roses. And then they started singing like canaries. They told me what the eighth graders are planning."

"No more suspense!" Jessi cried. "What are they planning?"

Frida leaned in and lowered her voice. "Grace found some blue spray paint in her Dad's workshop, so they're going to paint the roses that grow along the walkway to the Roses field," she said. "So that the red roses will be Kicks blue!"

I gasped. "But that's . . . that's vandalism! Isn't that just as bad as what the Rams tried to do to us?"

Frida shook her head. "I asked the same thing, but Jade says this isn't sabotage. It's just sending a message to the Roses not to mess with the Kicks. Grace told everyone that her dad played soccer in college, and they did stuff like that all the time, and nobody got in trouble."

I groaned. "That is just stupid! Of course they're going to get in trouble!"

"We should tell Coach Flores," Emma said.

"If we do that, Grace will still be in trouble," Jessi pointed out. "Maybe really big trouble. Maybe get-kicked-off-the-team trouble."

Without Grace or the other eighth graders on the team, we wouldn't have a chance at the play-offs. Our season would be over. Besides, even though Grace was difficult sometimes, I actually liked her. I knew she'd be devastated if she got kicked off the Kicks.

"Let me try to talk to her first," I said.

Jessi raised an eyebrow. "You? You're her number one enemy right now."

"No, the Roses are her number one enemy," I pointed out. "I'm still her co-captain. Let me try."

"It's planned for tonight, Devin," Frida said. "They're probably heading to the Roses field now."

"Oh no!" Emma wailed. "What should we do?"

Zoe took out her phone. "I have an idea," she said. "Sometimes it helps to have an older sister."

# CHAPTER FOURTEEN

"So let me get this straight," Zoe's sister Jayne said as she drove us to the Roses field in her car. "Some members of your team are about to do something stupid, and you want to stop them?"

"That's about right," Zoe said.

Zoe had asked Jayne to come pick us up. We'd told Mrs. Dukes that Jayne was taking us for ice cream, and when she had pointed out that five of us could not fit into the car safely, Jessi had agreed to stay behind. I had waved to her from the car, nervous about what was about to go down.

"It should be fairly simple," Frida said. "There shouldn't be anybody at the field at this time of night. The eighth graders said they were meeting at eight thirty. We should be just in time to stop them from painting the roses blue."

"That's a dumb thing to do," Jayne said, snapping her

gum. She had Zoe's blue eyes and blond hair, but her hair was long and straight, with long bangs. "You think you can stop them?"

"I'm not sure," I admitted. "But we have to try."

We rode in silence, and arrived at the Santa Flora Middle School field a few minutes later. Because the school teams were called the Roses, the walkway to the field was lined with rosebushes.

"Park on the street, not in the parking lot," Zoe said. "We don't want them to see us coming."

Jayne parked under a tree and turned off her lights.

"I'm going to go alone," I said. "If we get caught, it's not worth all of us getting in trouble."

"That's fine with me," Emma said, and I could tell she was nervous about the whole thing.

I got out and walked down the darkened path. I could see five girls huddled by the rosebushes, and as I got closer, I could make them out: Grace, Megan, Anjali, Jade, and Gabriela.

*At least it's not all of them*, I thought with some relief.

Then I heard Grace's voice. "Taylor? Is that you?"

I cleared my throat nervously. "No. It's Devin."

"What are you doing here?" Grace snapped.

I had reached them by now, and I took a deep breath. "I came to talk to you. I know the Roses are being jerks. And I'm sorry if my helping Sasha made it worse. But if you spray paint those roses blue, everyone will know it was the Kicks. And we could get in big trouble."

"We're not hurting anybody, or anything," Grace replied. "The paint will wash off. And nobody will be able to prove who did it."

"Exactly," I said. "So they'll blame the whole team. We might even get suspended from playing. Think about it!"

Gabriela bit her lip. "Devin's got a point. I didn't think of that."

"Yeah," Jade agreed.

"No, she's wrong," Megan said. "They can't suspend all of us if they can't prove anything." She picked up a spray can. "Come on. Let's do this."

Grace looked at me. "Unless you're planning on ratting us out, Devin?"

"No," I said quickly. "That's why I came, instead of calling Coach Flores."

"Just keep quiet about it, and we'll all be fine," Megan added.

Suddenly we were blinded by headlights. Too stunned to run, we all stood there, like deer.

"What's going on here, girls?"

The headlights dimmed, and a woman stepped out of the vehicle. It looked like the Roses' coach!

"Nothing," Grace said quickly. "We were just leaving."

The woman walked closer to us. It was definitely Coach Doyle. "Please wait," she said, and then she nodded toward Megan. "Is that spray paint?"

Megan's boldness left her. "Yes, ma'am," she said, and then she handed it to the coach, who squinted at it.

"Blue paint," she said, and then a look of recognition dawned on her face. She sighed. "Oh no. Are you girls from Kentville? I'm Coach Doyle." She shook her head. "This is very disappointing."

"We're really sorry," Grace said. "Can't we just go?"

Coach Doyle shook her head. "I think I should call your coach and let her know what her team is up to."

"But we're not up to anything!" Grace protested. "We haven't done a thing!"

"So you just came to stroll around the Roses field, in the dark, carrying blue spray paint?" Coach Doyle asked, and Grace stared at the ground.

I had broken out in a sweat. My throat felt dry. My stomach was doing flip-flops. Coach Doyle took out her phone, and then she looked at me.

"I'd like to tell Coach Flores which of her students are here," she said. "What's your name, and is there anything you'd like to explain?"

My head felt fuzzy. Now I was in trouble, just like the others! And all I'd been doing was trying to stop them! But I knew I couldn't tell Coach Doyle that. I was with my team, and teams stuck together.

"Devin Burke, ma'am," I replied. "And, um, no, there's nothing to explain."

To my surprise, Grace stepped forward.

"Devin shouldn't be in trouble for this," she said. "She heard about what we were going to do and came here to stop us. We were just going to paint the roses blue, that's all."

Coach Doyle looked at me. "Devin, can I assume that someone drove you here?"

I nodded silently.

"Then you may go," she said. "But next time let your coach deal with issues like this, okay?"

"Yes, I will," I said, and I flashed Grace a grateful look before running back to Jayne's car.

"What happened?" Emma squealed as I climbed into the backseat. "We saw a car pull up!"

"It was the Roses' coach," I reported. "I'm not sure what she was doing at the field, but she caught everyone before they sprayed the flowers. And she's calling Coach Flores."

"Oh no!" Emma cried.

"But she let you go?" Zoe asked.

"That's the crazy thing," I said. "Grace told her I was trying to stop them. She stood up for me."

"So I guess your Grace problem is solved, then," Frida said.

"Maybe," I agreed. "But I don't know what's going to happen to the others."

"Who was there?" Zoe asked.

"Grace, Megan, Anjali, Jade, and Gabriela," I said. "I think they're all in big trouble."

Then my phone beeped with a message from Jessi.

WHAT IS HAPPENING? I need 2 no!

Long story, I typed back. I am fine. But Grace + 4 caught by Roses' coach.

Noooooooooo! What about game 2morrow?

I don't know, I replied.

"Bummer," Jayne said from the driver's seat, with another snap of her gum. "So, what next? Do you guys need to stop a bank robbery? Thwart an alien takeover?"

"No, but that would be fun," Frida said.

"Could you please take us home?" I asked. "We've got a big game tomorrow."

Then everyone got quiet, because we were all thinking the same thing. We hoped we were going to have a game the next day! Who knew what Coach Flores was going to do?

# CHAPTER FIFTEEN

I got up extra early on Saturday morning—I think it was because I was so nervous. I went on a morning run, took a shower, and then ate a bowl of oatmeal, even though it was a warm, sunny morning. I loved the energy burst I got from oatmeal on the morning of a game, and it didn't totally fill me up.

Then I got dressed for the game. I put on a pair of new blue-and-white-striped socks and slipped my lucky pink headband into my hair before running back downstairs. Mom, Dad, and Maisie were all wearing blue T-shirts.

"Everybody's coming?" I asked.

"Yes, the stars have aligned," Mom replied. "Your three biggest fans can all be there!"

"I'm her smallest fan," Maisie quipped.

Mom hugged her. "Yes, but you're growing fast, Maisie."

I was happy that everyone was coming, but I was also a

little worried. I still had no idea what Coach Flores might do, after Grace and the others had gotten caught the night before. I kept checking my phone for a group text announcing that the Kicks had been disqualified from the league, but nothing came.

"Devin, are you okay?" Dad asked. "You don't seem to have your usual game-day bounce."

I hesitated. I still hadn't told them anything that had happened the night before at the Roses field, but it wasn't like me to keep things from my parents.

"I'll tell you on the way," I said.

The mood in the car got pretty serious as I told the story of how I had tried to stop Grace and some of the other eighth graders from spraying the roses blue.

"Devin, Coach Doyle was right—you should have told Coach Flores. Or me or your dad," Mom said.

"I know," I said. "I just didn't want Grace to get in trouble."

"But she did anyway," Dad pointed out. "Remember that the next time you have to make a decision like this."

"I'm also not happy that you went to the Roses field at night without telling us," Mom said.

"Well, I told you that Jayne was driving us home," I said. "We just made a stop on the way."

Mom frowned. "*Hmph!* We'll talk about this more after the game."

I sat back in the seat and closed my eyes, grateful that Maisie had her headphones on. I knew she would have had a lot of obnoxious things to say about my situation.

We pulled into the parking lot by the field, and when I got out of the car, Mom hugged me, to my surprise. Then, still holding me by the arms, she pulled away from me and looked into my eyes.

"Devin, I'm very proud of you for trying to do the right thing," she said. "And I know that you're at an age when you're feeling your wings, and wanting to make your own decisions. Just remember that Dad and I are always here to help you make the best possible decisions that you can."

"I will," I promised.

She let go of me. "Now, go out there and win that game!"

I jogged out to the field, but Dad was right—I didn't have my usual bounce. And then when I saw Grace in jeans and a T-shirt instead of her uniform, I felt absolutely deflated. Something was definitely going on.

"Devin, can I talk to you?" she asked.

"Sure," I said.

Grace took a deep breath. "Listen," she began. "I owe you an apology. I shouldn't have given you such a hard time for helping Sasha. And I'm glad you tried to stop us last night. You were right. So, thanks."

"It's okay," I said. "But what happened to you guys? Are you off the team?"

Grace shook her head. "No, just suspended for one game. Coach Doyle and Coach Flores agreed that was fair."

I let out a huge sigh. "Whoa. I'm so glad. I mean, it

stinks that you're suspended for a game. But I'm glad you're still on the team."

The other Kicks were starting to enter the field. I could see a few girls whispering and talking. Word must have gotten around about what had happened.

"Megan, Gabriela, Jade, and Anjali are all going to be in the stands today, cheering everybody else on," Grace said. "I asked Coach if I could talk to the team first and explain things, and she said yes."

I imagined having to face the whole team and admit that I had made a huge mistake. "That won't be easy."

"Yeah, but I'm a co-captain," she said. "So, you know, I've got to do it."

I nodded, because I understood exactly what she meant.

"I'm sorry I didn't realize how bad things were between you and Ashley of the Roses," I said. "She doesn't seem very nice."

"She's not, but I let her get to me, and that's my own fault," Grace replied. "You probably know this already, Devin, but I'm very competitive. Soccer is my life. I don't want to just do this for fun. I want to do it when I'm out of school. I want to go pro."

"I've been thinking about that too," I admitted.

"Yeah, but it's been messing with my head," Grace said. "I thought that in order to go pro, I always had to be on a winning team. That helps, but that's not all of it. I need to always play my best. And I can't let dumb insults get to me. I almost ruined everything, just because it bugs me when Ashley calls me 'Gross' instead of 'Grace.'"

"Yeah, when she goes low, you gotta go high," I said, and she smiled. "And also, you are on a winning team. And we're going to keep winning."

"I know you can do it today," Grace said. "Even without the five of us. We did great that day when everybody was sick."

Then she looked around. "I guess I'd better do this."

I followed her over to Coach Flores, and the coach called the team together.

"Team, I have some news," Coach said. "Grace, Megan, Jade, Anjali, and Gabriela are suspended from today's game. And Grace is going to tell you why."

I could see a tiny bit of fear in Grace's eyes, but she stepped forward and explained everything that had happened the night before. Everybody started whispering.

"I let this team down, and I'm sorry," Grace said. "And today you'll be playing five players short, and that's my fault. But I know you can beat the Panthers without us. You can do it if you remember that we're a team. We're all on the same side."

Grace smiled at me, and I smiled back.

"Now, Devin, it's time for a sock swap!" Grace said.

"Right!" I replied. "Everybody in a circle!"

We ran and sat down in the grass and took off our cleats. Jessi sat next to me, and I passed her my blue-and-white-striped sock.

"Well, that worked out okay, I guess," she remarked.

"Yeah," I agreed, and then I looked across the circle, where Zoe and Emma were cracking up.

"Pickles, Emma? Seriously? I can't go out there wearing a pickle sock!" Zoe complained, giggling.

"Of course you can! Pickles are good luck!" Emma replied.

"Says who?" Zoe asked.

"Says . . . I don't know. But it's true!" Emma said. "Anyway, who doesn't like pickles?"

"I guess it *all* worked out okay," I said, tying my shoe, "except for one thing."

"What's that?" Jessi asked.

"We haven't beaten the Panthers yet!" I jumped up. "Kicks, huddle!"

We got into a circle, and each one of us put our right hand in the middle.

"Goooooooooo, Kicks!"